The Dating Contract

The Dating Contract

A Last Girls Standing Romance

Stacey Agdern

The Dating Contract
Copyright© 2024 Stacey Agdern
Tule Publishing First Printing, March 2024

The Tule Publishing, Inc.

First Publication by Tule Publishing 2024

Cover design by ebooklaunch

ISBN: 978-1-962707-17-6

Chapter One

THE BRIGHT SUNLIGHT of a June morning reflected against the large expanse of the Manhattan convention center. The building, as per usual during a convention, was wrapped in signs and draped in lights.

But this was different.

This time, the signs and the lights all said, 'The New York Wedding Extravaganza' and all of it—the building, the signs, the lights and the convention it signified—was the bane of Leah Nachman's existence.

She didn't have a problem with weddings so to speak. What she did have a problem with, was the vibe emanating from the building she was about to enter. Even the air in the parking lot was nervous, excited, high-strung and tied so tightly she could barely breathe.

Not to mention the sheer numbers of people preparing to fill the facility, packed so closely she could barely lift an arm to adjust her sunglasses. And they were all dressed in various shades of white and pink and black and blue, bright enough to burn her eyeballs behind her sunglasses.

Only for her beloved older sister would Leah brave this

disaster. "Why, again, isn't Naomi here?"

Her sister lifted her gaze from the engagement ring occupying real estate on her left hand. "She's not just our cousin, she's a paid event planner working with clients who aren't us. And she figured, as my sister and maid of honor, that you'd be able to walk me through my agenda."

The agenda.

Settled into a three-hole blue ombré plastic binder were thick stapled packets filled with maps, schedules and notes about the vendors that only a project manager, like her sister, would love.

"So," Judith continued, touching her phone screen before lifting it up so Leah could see it. "You have an email now with calendar entries and their corresponding alarms that will go off for events I want to see if possible."

Leah's phone confirmed the receipt of the email with a buzz. "Got it," she said, aware the agenda had also found its way onto her phone.

For a second, Judith looked up, and Leah could see a question in her sister's eyes. "Fine?"

Leah knew that no matter what she said, Judith wouldn't pull the plug on this adventure. If this was a normal situation, Leah would even be thrilled her sister was focused on something *she* wanted.

But this wasn't normal. And all she could say was "Fine."

Judith nodded and Leah once again saw the flash of a question in her sister's eyes before it dissipated. "Let's do this."

Feeling pulled by the inevitable, Leah squared her shoulders, adjusted her entry tag and followed her sister into the building.

SAMUEL LEVINE WAS under the impression that without bad luck, he'd have none. Because otherwise, he never would have gotten the call from his older brother and business manager that morning, telling him his presence was needed.

"Even without your facial hair, you're still the face of your business."

Samuel sighed. Not every young single male sofer writing ketubahs and mezuzahs was searching for an opportunity to write one for himself. "I thought they came to me for my calligraphy."

Aaron shook his head. "Nope. Your jawline is sharper than any z you've ever written, and those brown eyes are more magnetic than your ink."

Samuel let that pass without comment; the whole 'hot sofer' thing had been Aaron's idea after all. But soon enough, the booth was set up in the usual manner. Aaron would station himself at the side, speaking to the people who approached and organizing business, and he'd be a bit further inside behind a table with pens, quills, ink, sheets of paper and a task list.

Not that he'd get anything done. It was just always better

to look like he was busy, or have something there that would allow him *to* be busy. Just in case.

"Ready?"

He settled into the chair and nodded. "Yep."

And as the clock struck ten, the hall was full of the sound of chatter, and the clatteof footsteps, which signified the rapid formation of lines.

"Hi," said the first woman in the queue. "I want a mezuzah and a date."

Somehow he managed to convince her and three other women that he wasn't interested, and told a man that he didn't want to make his future husband jealous no matter how many items he purchased.

The next customer came up to him with a big smile on her face. "Do you know Melanie Gould?"

He shook his head. "I don't," he'd said.

"But he—" the woman pointed at Aaron, who was smiling and already talking to someone else "—said you did something for her?"

That was when Samuel nodded, and the information clicked in his head. Whether it was a deliberate misunderstanding or that of a general kind, the problem was obvious. "My lettering did feature on some of these—" he pointed to the poster display behind him "—for the Goldstone saga series, which was based on Melanie Gould's books. And some of my work was even in the show, but I've never met her."

"See," another woman said, brown eyes filled with the look that came with an explanation made and ignored multiple times. "He doesn't know her. Like I told you."

"But I want to make the poster my ketubah theme," the first person said, clearly the bride. "I want my first child to be named Moshe after the first hero in the series and…"

"Tell her it's a horrible idea to live your marriage like it's one of your favorite books."

This line of conversation wasn't new, but he'd been dealing with it more and more recently. Whether it was the *hot sofer* thing or the push for the LivePix series, it didn't matter.

But he wasn't good at the delicate maneuvering a situation like this needed; his brother, glib and socially gifted, was the front man. And unfortunately, Aaron was doing his networking and negotiations and holding court in his usual spot.

Which meant defusing the tension, in a way that wouldn't end up with him fighting copyright infringement, was up to him.

Task clear, Samuel pulled himself together and smiled. "Listen," he said, searching for the right words, "I can absolutely create a ketubah based on a combination of your and your future spouse's interests, something to build a future on. I can even sign a poster for you."

"Wait," the first woman said. "You can sign a poster for me?"

He nodded, glad he'd managed to find something that

would calm the situation. "I can absolutely sign a poster for you."

"Good." And then a grin from the bride, a sigh from what looked like her long-suffering companion. "Sign a poster and I'll get a ketubah and a mezuzah."

And as he signed the poster, watching the women head over toward his brother, there was a strange feeling developing in what felt like his stomach.

It wasn't breakfast or lack thereof, and it wasn't nerves.

So what was it? What was going on? He definitely needed to find out.

"WHAT'S YOUR FIRST stop?" Leah asked as they made their way inside, past security checks and the ticket checks. This was Judith's show, and as she reminded herself, Leah was just along for the ride.

"Ketubahs," Judith replied.

Fair enough.

Ketubahs were the one thing required for a Jewish wedding after all. And they were art—calligraphy, paintings—which meant work went into finding the right artist. And so Leah put on her maid of honor hat and followed her sister up the escalator.

"This way," Judith said.

After a while of perusing the booths, she heard her sister's question. "Anything?"

If Leah was going to be honest, there wasn't anything. But this wasn't Leah's show. It was Judith's. Which meant she had to make it clear where she stood while interpreting the situation. "No. But more importantly, do you see anything? This is for you."

But Judith didn't have a poker face, and Leah didn't have to read her sister's mind to know that she'd only asked the question to confirm she'd seen nothing that belonged on the wall of whatever residence she'd share with Asher. "No."

So they continued to walk through, when all of a sudden, Judith stopped. Leah watched as her sister extended her arm and then her index finger toward one of the booths. "What the hell is this?"

Leah followed the direction her sister was pointing in, only to see a line.

A never-ending line of people.

She was used to seeing lines outside, and in very few booths on the main floor, like the cake-tasting areas, or some of the shoe or jewelry designers.

But here? Where the ketubah section was? "What the hell is right!"

And then Leah took in her sister's expression, trying to discern what was going through Judith's mind.

That way meant disaster.

No. Absolutely not. "We're not waiting on that line," Leah said, making it very clear to her sister that this was a line she wasn't crossing.

"Wouldn't even think of it," Judith said, sounding chastised. Because of course her sister had no poker face and it was very obvious to Leah that Judith *had* thought of suggesting they stand on the line.

Instead, as if Judith was changing tactics, she looked toward the crowd. "What's going on?"

"The hot sofer," said the woman closest to them, or rather the woman standing in front of them.

"I wouldn't mind if he, you know, made *me* a ketubah," said the man who'd gotten behind them.

Because she had followed Judith, and now Leah and her sister were, in fact, waiting on the line.

Of course they were.

But she'd heard many things in her lifetime (she was a sports agent after all) but this? Well. This took the cake.

"Are you waiting for a consult?" Judith asked, because it seemed they were actually going to get a consult with this '*hot sofer*.'

Whoever he was.

"I just want him to sign my...well..." the young woman said, pointing to what she'd been carrying; it was rolled up and secured with a rubber band. Leah figured it had to be some kind of poster.

"So you just want his autograph?" Leah clarified.

The woman nodded. "Yes."

"Got it. And," Judith ventured, not to be deterred by

autograph seekers, "if you do want a consult?"

"His business manager," the gentleman chimed in, "is over there. He's the one inside the line."

There were many sofers who had business managers on site at the convention. With no reason for...lines and this kind of disaster.

But she followed Judith anyway, as her sister made a beeline toward the area where the business manager was supposed to be. Supposed to, because if she was running this appearance, she'd be nowhere near this...*mishegas.*

"Judith Nachman!"

Her sister turned at the sound of the voice, which was familiar in a way that made Leah nervous.

"Aaron!!" Judith yelled, in what clearly seemed like recognition.

Wait. Aaron...Levine?

Judith was a year younger than Aaron Levine. As they started to talk, Judith enthusiastically describing how excited she was for the wedding, the bright tones of her sister's voice wreaked havoc through Leah's already messed-up head...

"Oh," Aaron said, "my brother can totally make your ketubah!"

Aaron had one brother.

And the less Leah said about him, the better.

"Really?" Judith squealed, and yes, *actually* squealed.

But the squeal filled Leah with dread. "Um," Leah managed, wanting to put the brakes on this impending disaster as quickly as she possibly could.

Unfortunately, it seemed the train had left the station, as her sister wasn't paying attention to anything. She was focused on the ketubahs and…

"SAMUEL!" Aaron's voice rang through the confusion in the convention hall.

Oh. God.

If Leah could have walked away or done anything other than stand there, she would have.

But she couldn't.

So she pulled her professional-agent, don't-mess-with-me mask on—shoulders back, eyes focused, jaw stiff before turning in the direction of Aaron's voice.

And of course Aaron caught her gaze and was now pointing.

The eyes were what she saw first; the same chocolate brown she spent high school drowning in. There was a slight grayish tint to his sideburns and the slightest trace of razor burn on his cheeks that hid cheekbones sharper than any word he'd ever uttered in her defense.

He wasn't the same; nobody stayed the same after almost twenty years.

But in his eyes, Leah could see the boy who broke her heart all those years ago.

Damn him.

"Leah."

Even now, Samuel Levine's voice wrapped around her in

ways she didn't want to succumb to. But she shoved her emotions deep down inside of her, settled into a neutral state as she matched his glance with her own. "Samuel."

It became a contest, and she refused to back down. *Never let them see you sweat*, they said.

Well.

She wasn't letting him see her blink.

"Leah."

She heard the under-the-breath reprimand in her sister's voice. But Leah wasn't budging.

"Who is she? Who is she?"

It started as a whisper, but the noise became louder; she could presume the cacophony of voices came from the line, a crowd of fascinated bystanders.

But all she cared about was making him blink first.

Samuel's long lashes came down only for a second.

And yet, she could see the tension in his throat.

What was going on?

"She's my girlfriend."

Leah bit her lip to keep from screaming. Forced herself to stay still to keep from racing to erase the space between them and shaking him.

Which was when she saw the desperation in his eyes.

"Please."

If it had been anywhere else, she would have turned away or thrown something.

But she'd never hear the end of it from her sister, and if

she had to really think about it, she liked the idea of him owing her. Not to mention Aaron was clearly shit at crowd control, something that someone trading on the name *the hot sofer* desperately needed.

So she assessed the room, and then headed to the space by Samuel's side, right behind the table.

And suddenly, the line was shorter, presumably leaving only the people who were there for Samuel's art, not his face.

Out of the corner of her eye, she could see Judith talking with Aaron.

"Do you want me to do your sister's ketubah? I'm assuming that's why she's talking to Aaron?"

His voice broke the silence she was trying to create. Not to mention the way his voice still did things to her all those years later was still a large problem. But she was used to wearing masks of indifference. "Why would I care?" she asked. "Exactly?"

"I figured that, you know, because you're here, that your opinions matter."

She raised an eyebrow. "Why do you think she wants one of your ketubahs?"

"Because she and my brother seem to be negotiating one."

Which was a detail she should have paid attention to, except she hadn't. But in the end, the only opinion that mattered was her sister's. And if she needed to educate Samuel she would. "It doesn't matter. She's the bride."

And as her sister negotiated a ketubah with Aaron, she was stuck there. Playing public girlfriend for Samuel, one bad decision leading to another.

And now she was stuck.

Dammit.

ONE MINUTE SAMUEL was navigating through the process of talking to people and autographing posters, the next he'd turned toward the sound of his brother's voice only to see Judith Nachman's profile.

Which meant that the blue eyes staring at him could only belong to one person. The familiar shade of blue he'd tried to duplicate in ink, the very particular brown of her hair he saw in every single calligraphy brush he used.

Leah.

Her features had come to life with age as if she'd escaped from a cryogenic container. She was beautiful; she'd always been, but now? Now she was perfect. She was just as transfixed as he was, it seemed, until the moment he watched her draw herself inwards, as if she'd flipped a switch.

Which meant he was now in...of all things...a staring contest?

Samuel wasn't sure, but what he did see was movement, anticipation in the eyes of at least the first person on line in front of him. Which meant the noise he'd started to hear were whispers of questions that got louder and louder.

And yet despite all of that, all he could see was Leah. Standing there. And whether it was panic, delusion or hope, he wasn't sure. All the same, he blurted out the first answer to the question that came to his mind.

"She's my girlfriend."

And now Leah Nachman stood next to him, watching the now much smaller line clear out.

"Fine," she'd said, answering his question about whether she minded if he made her sister's ketubah. "It's my sister's ketubah, not mine. Your business, your choice."

"So again," he said, realizing he'd pulled her into drama she didn't want, "does it bother you?"

"I'm not the one in the market for a ketubah," she snapped, before pausing as if she'd realized he wasn't trying to cause trouble. "Or a boyfriend. You need better crowd control."

He'd never been more confused, but he'd take it. "Okay?"

"I'm serious," she said, shaking her head as if she was judging his performance. "If you're doing this *hot sofer* thing, you need better crowd control."

That again. That idea, marketing plan, whatever it was. Aaron's not so brilliant idea had gotten him publicity and more commissions, but not the kind of attention he wanted. It had, in fact, become a nightmare.

But for some reason he felt it was important to make it

clear to Leah that the title of *hot sofer* wasn't something he wanted. Not that she'd change her opinion of him so easily. But he felt she needed to know. "I'm not *doing* it. Not my idea. It just is."

"Whatever," Leah said, as if she was closing a door. Of course his thoughts didn't matter to her.

"Whosever idea it was," she continued, "it was a marketing choice that creates crowds. You need to *deal* with crowds."

He blinked. What? "Are you saying you'll... Are you offering to fix the problem you think I have?"

She shook her head. He wasn't that lucky. "My obligation to clean up your mess ended a long time ago, if it ever existed in the first place."

Right.

Ages ago.

When he'd been a dumb high school kid who broke her heart.

And according to the script, after she uttered that truism, she'd leave and they'd be done.

Except she didn't leave.

"Once my sister finishes organizing her ketubahs with your brother, I'm gone."

That was the addition to the script he'd forgotten; she wasn't here at all of her own volition. Not in the building, not at the expo, not at his booth. But all he could say was: "Fair enough."

"You have no poker face," she continued, as if her entire purpose was to examine him and pick out his faults or analyze his business practices for potential problems. "You need one."

He did. Need one. But that was what Aaron was for, right?

Or what he was supposed to be for at least. Public-facing glib businessperson, protecting the ridiculously strange sofer who happened to have a nice face.

"Anyway," she said. "I think my sister has a huge list of things to do, so we should probably move on."

"I won't keep you," he said.

Even though he wanted to.

Even though he wanted to tease her, to give her reason to stay and talk, a buzzer went off on her phone; she lifted it up and he saw something about a cake.

"The cake-tasting area's been busy the entire time," he said. "If you have a particular cake you want to taste…?"

"We do," she said, taking the information as gratefully as he gave it.

"Then," he said, deciding give her an out of some sort, "you'll probably have to, you know, head over there soon."

Leah nodded. He could see the surprise in her expression, as if she hadn't expected to have this kind of interaction. "Probably sooner than that. Thank you for the advice."

"Turnabout is fair play," he replied. "Poker face and

crowd control."

She nodded again, the expression on her face as if he was reminding her of something she'd prefer to forget. "Right. Bye."

"More like 'see you around,'" he replied. "Because ketubah."

"Right," she said as if she'd forgotten her sister was negotiating with his brother. "One of my maid of honor tasks. So, I guess it is 'see you around.'"

And as he watched Leah walk away, he wondered what else would happen now that she was back in his life. More importantly, he wondered what he'd do to keep her there.

Chapter Two

LEAH HAD NO idea what had come over her. What had possessed her to go along with Samuel's random scheme?

She hadn't come up with any conclusion when her buzzer rang.

She got up from the couch, crossed the room and looked through the peephole.

Naomi?

What was her cousin doing here?

But all the same, she unlocked and opened the door, letting her cousin in. "Hi?"

"You are the talk of the family group chat," Naomi said. "But we need to walk and talk because we are on a mission."

Leah blinked. "Uhhh…"

You and I are going to a photography exhibit," Naomi said. "It's an opening at a gallery downtown."

None of this made sense. "You don't even like photography at galleries. Why are we doing this?"

"Wedding stuff."

Which made sense; except… "What…I thought I was

done with that for the day."

Naomi suddenly looked as if she'd rehearsed the story she was about to tell a billion times on the way. And Leah wasn't going to keep her cousin from delivering a performance. "Judith got a favor from her boss, which means we have tickets to go see the opening of an exhibit put together by the guy who she might want to take the wedding photos."

Judith, her boss and his legendary favors were enough to make Leah lose her mind. This was…normal in the scheme of things but still strange. Especially after Judith had headed back to Briarwood after the expo, having sworn wedding duties were over for the day. "Okay…but tonight?"

"Yeah," Naomi replied. "Friends and family. Opening preview night, which means a better chance of both talking to the photographer and seeing the photos."

"And why am I coming? I was on duty all day. I deserve the night to sleep."

"You're both maid of honor and *here*."

Here was her Manhattan apartment, more convenient than Naomi's place in Queens. "That makes sense, as to why you're stopping by but…"

"This is your responsibility, Maid of Honor," Naomi said with a laugh.

"She told me I was done for the day," Leah repeated. "And she's the bride, shouldn't her opinion matter?"

"Hers does. And you're done with her, but not with me. Ersatz planner and cousin reporting for duty. Also, it seems you have a lot to tell me."

"About?"

From the look in Naomi's eyes, it was clear to Leah that Judith had said something in the group chat about the bridal expo.

Which meant that Leah was in trouble.

SAMUEL WAS EXHAUSTED.

End of day at the expo was weird and Aaron still hadn't stopped talking about the moment where Samuel had called Leah his girlfriend.

"She said our crowd control stinks." He shook his head. "Like a sofer needs crowd control."

"Someone who uses their looks as a way to drive their sales needs crowd control," his brother had quipped as they finished loading out. "Also, you're a multimedia artist, so you're going to get cross-pollination."

Aaron had been joking but it was true. And yes, the marketing campaign had been Aaron's idea in the first place, but it still affected how he was expected to be in public.

Which was something he was thinking about on the way to meet his mentor, Liam Hernandez, at a gallery opening for a photographer he'd been following. He and Liam had been paired up since Samuel had finished design school, which had a pretty big blessing; Liam was a supportive mentor who understand what Samuel wanted out of his career.

"Looking forward to seeing you," Liam had said in the phone call that got him out of his apartment after load-out knowing he had all of Monday to relax. "We're going to have a lot to talk about in the next few days."

And Samuel *was* excited; there was something about knowing Leah could be back in his life that made him…exhilarated. Not to mention, he decided as he got off the subway and made his way through the streets of Lower Manhattan, there was something in the air and he didn't mean the heat.

He wasn't sure what exactly it was, but as he arrived at the door, he was ready for anything. "Levine," he said to the gentleman behind the podium. "I'm here to see…"

"Sammy," his mentor said with a grin before turning toward the guy in control of the line. "Liam Hernandez, on the list. He's with me. Glad you came."

Samuel focused on Liam's face instead of the slowly growing crowd. "Me too," he said.

"How did your thing go?"

Liam's question was genuine and thinking of it made Samuel realize how tired he actually was. "Good, I think," he said. "Met people, signed things, and got some commissions."

"Still enjoying yourself?"

That was the real question, and despite how tired he was,

the answer was easy. “That side, doing that kind of work is challenging and I’m enjoying it. But I also want to keep doing posters, and things like that.”

Liam nodded. “You want to stretch your horizons, widen your comfort zone, and grow as an artist, hm?”

That was it in a nutshell. Liam always got it; he knew how to speak Samuel. “Yep,” he told his mentor. “That’s it exactly. I don’t want to stay the same, don’t want to do the same thing.”

“Well then,” Liam replied, a smile as large as the Cheshire cat’s. “We’ve got people to meet and art to see.”

Bolstered by his mentor’s approval, he followed Liam deeper into the crowd and the show. Things were happening and he was looking forward to whatever opportunities came his way.

“SO,” NAOMI SAID as Leah began to get ready, “what the hell is up with your sister?”

Which was not the question Leah had expected to hear, but grateful for small miracles she replied, “Kool-Aid. My uber-focused, rational, professional sister has been in a relationship. Which means she has decided that everybody else needs to be in one.” She paused and stared at the black blazer she was going to wear. “Or were you asking about something else?”

Her cousin laughed. "Right. Luckily I don't have that problem."

"Just wait," Leah said as she walked into the living room. "Liv will fall hard and it will all be over for you."

Leah couldn't help but snicker as her cousin turned incredulous. "Nope. My sister is in love with being in office. Love isn't happening to *her* anytime soon. But..."

Leah raised an eyebrow. "Yes?"

"What's the deal with you and Samuel Levine?"

The inevitable had arrived; the escape she thought she'd had was no longer. "Do you want the short version or the long one?"

Leah waited as shock colored her cousin's features.

"You mean there's a story?"

Naomi loved her stories of course, but then Leah remembered she was being dragged to an opening. "What time is this thing?"

"You're admitting to a story."

Leah grabbed her purse in frustration. "I'm admitting to a need for context. You're asking me about Samuel out of the blue, which means there's a reason. Most likely, it's because Judith said something...because that's the first thing you asked me."

Deduction was easy and her cousin was flummoxed.

"You're scary."

"You remember what I do for a living," Leah replied as she headed toward the door. "It's my job to get these details.

So what did she say and what do you want to know?"

"She said something about high school," Naomi said, delivering the goods just like Leah thought, "but also I've heard you're his girlfriend?"

Which means Judith gave a mess of details and Naomi needed everything.

Which sucked.

"We dated in high school," Leah confirmed, reluctantly passing along the information. "You remember how I was sobbing into my Passover wine our senior year?"

A shock of recognition crossed Naomi's face as Leah opened the door. "The guy who didn't stand up for you?"

Which was a pretty good explanation of an incident where a sixteen-year-old girl had to hear her boyfriend sitting silently and even laughing at the cruel jokes made at her expense. "Yeah. He was Mr. Spineless."

"So the *hot sofer* who is making your sister's ketubahs is the infamous Mr. Spineless all grown up?" Naomi shook her head as Leah closed the door behind her. "Wow."

Wow was an understatement. "It's something," she said.

"Well," Naomi replied as they headed toward the elevator. "Now that you've given me the info on the ketubah writer, let's head out on the town and get your sister a photographer."

As they headed out, the nagging feeling inside of her was back. The last time it showed up, she ran into Samuel for the first time in a long time. The very last thing she needed was a repeat.

He wouldn't show up at a photography show the same day of the wedding expo, right?

Chapter Three

"SO," LIAM SAID with a smile. "How's it been going?"

The exhibition had been going on for a while, and it had been…fun. "Good," Samuel said. "Photographs have been some of his best, and it's been nice, you know, being around creative people."

"Glad you enjoyed seeing the photographs," Liam said and laughed, and there was a slight touch of reprimand in his mentor's voice that Samuel didn't get. "But I meant the people."

Which made sense. "Well," he began, trying to explain himself, "I…"

Liam shook his head, stopping any explanation he could possibly make. "Didn't bring you here just for you to stare at photographs, you know."

He didn't know—that was news to him. "What?"

His mentor clapped his shoulder. "I know," Liam said as he looked into the crowd for someone, "pretty much everybody here."

It wasn't a surprise; Liam had always been well connected. Which meant Samuel should take advantage of the position he'd been put in. "Anybody in particular that I should say hello to?"

Liam nodded, pointing into the crowd. "Oliver Goldsmith."

Oliver was an artist he admired. "The painter Oliver Goldsmith?"

"He and I went to school together," Liam replied. "He's a good contact for you as you keep your feet in two different areas of lettering."

Right. Oliver, aside from being a painter, was also a trained colorist—another very specialized area of comic art. "Okay." He paused. "Where is he?"

Liam pointed to the other side of the room, to one of the only other people wearing a collared shirt. "Him."

Samuel nodded. "Okay."

Liam, clearly not convinced that Samuel would listen, and right about it, laughed. "Let's go over there."

As he followed his mentor into the small group of people, Samuel knew that everything was about to change.

"SO," NAOMI SAID as they got out of the taxi a block away from the gallery. "Now tell me about what has everybody buzzing."

Leah blinked. "Everybody?"

"Party planners, brides. The expo."

Leah sighed as she started to walk down the street, regretting her decision to wear heels. Apparently her cousin's perception of who 'everybody' was changed with the minute. "What exactly are you talking about? I told you the story."

"I know the context. But what's the deal with him being your boyfriend now? Don't you not like him? Are we not supposed to like him?"

Leah desperately tried to stop herself from killing her cousin. "A one-time public stunt to fix the fact the man doesn't understand crowd control. Nothing more."

"Ooooh." Naomi shook her head as they stopped in front of the gallery. "Too hasty methinks."

"Sometimes words don't require much thought." Leah replied as she followed her cousin into the air-conditioned building.

"Says you who overthink everything," Naomi snorted. Not that her cousin had any right to judge. "That will be the day—when you say something you haven't rehearsed."

"Not me," Leah said as they headed to the podium holding the guest list.

"Naomi Nachman," her cousin said.

"Leah Nachman," Leah said following protocol. "My name may or may not be on the list."

"Enjoy," the security guard said as he waved them through.

And as she walked into the exhibit, once again, Leah felt something strange at the pit of her stomach. Once again she hoped the feeling didn't signify yet another entanglement with someone best left in the past.

SOMETIMES, SAMUEL FOUND himself in awe of his life and his surroundings. Two words to his mentor and there he was in deep conversation with Oliver Goldsmith, who had, by some strange twist of fate, possessed a mezuzah he'd made.

"Your stuff is the rage," Liam had said.

Which was news to him. He enjoyed himself, and worked as hard as he could. "I guess it shows when I love what I do?"

"And the posters for the Goldstone series," Oliver said. "The lettering was exquisite."

That was it. He was done. May his memory be a blessing. Then and there.

But he had to be cool and casual. "Means a lot coming from you."

Oliver smiled. "You're one of us," he said. "An artist on the rise. L'chaim."

Samuel, still stunned, lifted the glass of club soda Liam had snagged from a passing waiter, and clinked glasses with Liam and Oliver.

As he started to try and participate in the conversation, his brain gradually adjusting to what Oliver had said, he looked up and met Leah Nachman's eyes. This, he thought was going to be interesting.

Bashert. Fated.

THE EXHIBIT WAS filled with people of all sorts and framed photographs using different variants of light and scene. They were stunning.

"These are amazing," Naomi said.

They were. But seeing her jaded cousin amazed by something surprised Leah. "I don't have words," she said.

"Why?"

"Because you don't usually love photography."

"Photography is part of my makeup case set of skills," Naomi said, as if she'd given this explanation before. "It's not my job to take photographs, but I can recognize a good photographer when I see one. However..."

"Yes?"

Leah encouraged the extra commentary because she thought it was about the photography, but the look in Naomi's eyes should have convinced her otherwise. Mischief. Pure mischief.

"You sure the thing with *the hot sofer* was crowd control only?"

Upset. Ire.

Of course. "Oh my God," she said, trying not to yell. "You're as bad as Judith, not to mention it's out of nowhere."

"It's not out of nowhere," Naomi quipped back, as if her cousin was trying to find some justification. "We're here, after all, for Judith's wedding."

"Do you realize the headache Judith's wedding has been already?" The words flew out of her mouth and none of it was Naomi's fault, but her cousin got the brunt of it. "Sorry."

"It's fine," Naomi said, "but…um…"

"What?"

Leah followed her cousin's outstretched finger, only to realize the entire room was staring at her.

And of course the nasty feeling in the pit of her stomach had been right on target, as her gaze settled on Samuel Levine.

Good thing he was nice to look at, and once again his eyes pulled her in like tractor beams.

But this time?

This time she had a plan. Instead of letting herself fall into the black hole, she was going to be proactive. "I didn't realize my boyfriend would be here."

And without looking back at her cousin, she crossed the room, took Samuel by the arm, led him to the first door she saw and dragged him in behind her.

NORMALLY, SAMUEL WOULD have been thrilled to be dragged into a private room by Leah Nachman, but this. This was… "What?"

"Turnabout is fair play," she said, still gorgeous, still unapproachable.

"I don't… I mean…"

"Do you realize what my life has been like in the time since you announced to the wedding expo that I was your girlfriend?"

He shook his head; he'd been exhausted after setup and then ran here, so he hadn't heard anything about anything. "I don't. Can you enlighten me?"

He tried to be as earnest as possible; it was entirely possible she wouldn't believe him, but after a beat she nodded.

"Fine. My entire family wants to know what's up with us, my sister is giddy and apparently the wedding planning industry wants to know the identity of the *hot sofer's* girlfriend."

He could read the agitation in her movements, and it didn't bode well for anything. "I'm sorry."

"I'm a sports agent," she continued, lost in her own words. "I'm a professional. This…whatever it is can't continue."

"Well," he said, trying not to sound like he was adding to her difficulties or making this situation sound like it would be worse for him. "You just informed a bunch of New York's art circle, as well as my mentor, who works at BP comics, that I'm your boyfriend."

"And this isn't a problem for you?"

His first instinct was to say no, that maybe this whole thing was bashert, confirming they were tied together by threads, strings, or whatever plans drew people together. Why else would they run into each other now?

But he had to give her an answer. The silence between them had extended for too long. "It's a problem because it's caused you trouble."

"Diplomatic as always," she said.

What alternative did he have? "What do you want from me?"

"To fix this mess," she said. "I have an important meeting with the agency head on Tuesday and I don't need any more distractions."

Subtext—because you caused a big one already. "So what do you suggest I do about it?"

He watched her pace, watched the agent, the professional come to life underneath her skin. PR. Damage control. "I don't live that far from here. Take me home, or at least to the subway. Let's say our goodbyes."

He nodded, because it seemed like this was going to be an interesting ride.

Chapter Four

LEAH HAD NO idea what she'd been thinking. What she'd done the night before was a desperate play.

But agreeing to go bridesmaid dress shopping with Naomi while she was still trying to figure out where her life was, was practically inexcusable.

"You paying attention?"

Leah looked up at her cousin and the selection of dresses that were sitting in front of her. "I am," she said. "Enough to get the dress on and veto orange."

"Good," Naomi said. "So what exactly was going on last night? I thought the situation with the *hot sofer* was a combination of high school trauma and crowd control."

"I don't know what last night was," Leah said, trying for honesty. "Desperation."

"Fate."

Leah glared at her cousin. "I have no time for this."

"What do they say? What's meant to be will be?"

Leah rolled her eyes as she put on the next dress. "I look like a tomato in this dress," she said, glaring at the bright red concoction of lace and silk she wore. "If you say bashert, I will smack you."

"Well," Naomi said. "If it's right…"

"The only thing that's right for me," Leah said, "is the meeting I have with Bruck tomorrow."

"Meeting with the agency head, hm?" Naomi asked. "Asking for partnership?"

Leah nodded as she opened the dressing room door to display the red disaster for her cousin. "That's the plan. You?"

"Keep me posted, but take that ugly dress off. You do look like you belong in a lasagna. Once the wedding that kept me from that expo is over, I'll be able to give Judith more time and talk to my boss about more space and more responsibility."

Which was something her cousin had been promising for a while. She only hoped that Naomi meant it this time. But all she said, was: "Okay."

"Good." she replied. "Now try on the next dress."

SAMUEL ELECTED TO take refuge from the thoughts that still bombarded him on Monday morning by organizing supplies. It was a necessary job and yet kept him from deep thoughts. He was filling his third fountain pen when his phone buzzed. Lifting it up, he saw it was Liam.

He'd actually been half convinced Liam would never talk

to him again after he left the gallery with Leah out of nowhere last night. So it was a huge weight off his shoulders when he saw the number. "Glad to hear from you," he said.

"You're surprised?"

Samuel laughed. Which was probably better than diving deeply into some kind of apology for his behavior, and then decided to be honest. "I thought that after last night, the chances of this conversation happening were slim to none."

In reply, Liam laughed, which was a relief. "You're good at what you do," Liam said once he'd stopped laughing. "And I was wondering what those rumors about you having a girlfriend were about."

"We were high school sweethearts," he said, which was the easiest explanation he could come up with, yet it still sounded strange to his own ears.

"Nice. Bring her."

"Uh," he managed. "To what?"

"I'm hosting a party in a few weeks," Liam said. "It's fun. Actually, it's for Oliver."

"Really," Samuel said. "You're hosting a party for Oliver?"

"Yep." He could hear Liam move papers around in the background. "Isaac brought his wife to one of these shindigs before she married him. She bought me some cool notebooks."

Now it was Samuel's turn to laugh. "So you take credit for the matchmaking?"

"I take credit for making it clear to her what she was getting into with Isaac's friends," Liam clarified, sounding proud, as if he actually had done the matchmaking.

But all Samuel could say was, "Interesting. When is it?"

"I'll let you know. But that's not the reason I called."

"Oh? What's going on?"

"You have more space on your schedule for me? This time, slightly more professional?"

He laughed. "I always have space for you. What do you need?"

There was a long pause, and Samuel wondered what was going on. "A friend of mine asked me for a favor, so this one I owe you for if you're going to agree to do it."

Which sounded more interesting by the second; a commission possibly? But all he said was, "Okay?"

"Evan Lefkowitz is an old friend of mine."

He paused. He knew Liam was from Jersey but not much else. Connections were connections, worlds were small and people knew tons of people, but he wanted to make sure. "The Evan Lefkowitz who's runs Tzedakah Exchange?"

"Yes," Liam said with a laugh. "That Evan Lefkowitz. He had a wonderful phase where he picked grass while he was supposed to play goalie on our soccer team."

Having had a similar phase when he was about six, Samuel snorted. "That is amazing. So what's going on?"

"Evan is apparently involved with raising a charity event from the dead, and yes I'm dragging you with me. He needs some kind of design for the logo."

"Right," he managed, desperately trying to erase the image of a zombie charity gala from his head, attempting to focus on the most important part of what Liam was saying. "So you're taking me to a gala that needs a logo you want me to letter. Okay. So what's it for?"

"Women and girls and kids in sports," Liam began. "The thing was supposed to happen this past May, but the whole thing fell apart before Evan's girlfriend got involved. She was supposed to be honored, but as everything fell apart and she intervened, what she wanted was to honor an organization that was important to her."

Evan Lefkowitz's girlfriend was a hockey player. Did she know Leah? Was Leah her agent? Was this an organization that Leah was involved in? Was it a gala she'd go to?

Which meant he had to ask. "What's the organization?"

"The one being honored?"

He nodded, then remembered Liam couldn't see him. "Yeah. What organization is being honored?"

"It's this program out of an ice rink in Westchester? It's registered as a 4U girls' program, but they're not too tight about who signs up as long as they play by the program rules, you know? There are tutus and unicorn horns used apparently? So there needs to be some kind of unicorn with a formal tutu in the gala graphic."

All he could hear was a program for young kids playing hockey with unicorn horns. It sounded like something Leah would have loved when they were younger, and he'd bet she knew about it now. "That sounds great."

"Good to hear," Liam said "Because the plan is that I'm going to sketch it out and Oliver's going to color, of course, and then I want you to letter."

As he listened to Liam's particular ideas for lettering, he definitely thought something was at work. Something he couldn't quite figure out.

It was too early to say whether he thought it was bashert, but either way, he was going to have to figure out how to contact Leah without getting her deeper into the web they were weaving.

AS LEAH PREPPED her notes for the early morning meeting, she turned on one of her dramas as a bit of background noise.

She'd seen it millions of times before, but never tired of it. It was the story of two people who agreed to date for a contractually obligated period of time. They were boss and secretary, but as time went on, it was revealed that they shared a secret past. And as time went further on, they realized they'd been in love the entire time.

Childhood sweethearts only got together when they both had intestinal fortitude and grew together, matured together in the same direction.

But something was drawing her and Samuel back into the same orbit, and the last thing she wanted to do was to revisit her past. She didn't have the time to do that kind of emotional work.

But what about…fake dating? Contractual obligations, public appearances, dealing with her interfering family and whoever was driving him batty, all solved in one fell swoop.

And unlike the people in the drama, she was very well aware of what a disaster she and Samuel had been together. She'd be in no danger of being a fake-dating fail.

Perfect.

If anything was a sign she was going on the right path, it was the email sitting in her inbox from him saying they had to talk. She dashed off a quick reply with her cell number, asking him to call her at around five when she was finished at the office.

This, she decided as she watched the drama's hero impress the heroine's family by gathering clams on the beach, was going to be a walk in the park.

Chapter Five

THERE WAS SO much going through Samuel's head on Tuesday morning as he headed toward the subway. He hadn't fully processed the weekend's events, and he knew there'd be more when he saw his brother.

It was a quick walk to the office space his brother rented, and the summer air wasn't that oppressive yet. The air conditioning blasted out of the office building as he opened the door, making Samuel long for the sweatshirt he'd forgotten back in Queens.

But he now was in Manhattan, hoping his brother would be some degree of sane with the temperature. Unfortunately, the second he opened the door, all he saw was his brother, harried as usual in a sweater, random scattered scraps of paper all over his side of the office and at least three coffee cups. "You look like you belong in December," he said, still longing for his sweatshirt.

"Don't ask me to turn it down or turn on the heart. This is as warm as I could make it."

Which didn't bode well for him later. "Thanks," he said.

"I assume that thanks is for managing most of the aftermath of the expo yesterday."

Samuel looked up to see an expression on his brother's face that meant business. "How did it go?"

"Going through the information, I logged a few more ketubah commissions than normal, and some requested mezuzahs. You also got an email from the poster people."

The poster people—the company that had requested his services to letter the Goldstone Saga posters. Could they want another poster or—?

But all he said to his brother was: "Yeah?"

"They want you to sign the Goldstone posters at comic con, and gave you a pass for yourself and a guest. Tommy and I are busy."

Signing at comic con.

Wow.

Like the people who lettered for the comic publishers, like BP.

Wow.

But all he managed in front of his brother was: "Interesting. I'm in."

"Good. And yes. I saw the email about the logo. Some awards event."

Which meant Liam must have emailed his business email, and that meant it was serious. "Yeah. It's for Liam so I need to block time on my calendar. Any things I should watch out for?"

Aaron nodded. "One of the ketubahs has some interesting design notes, which are a little…bonkers even though I negotiated them down."

"Really?"

Aaron nodded. "You'll see it when you look through everything." And then he paused. "Not much else happened after the *hot sofer* announced he had a girlfriend. Especially fascinating was that the girl is Leah Nachman."

"I…" He paused, doing his best to explain the situation to his brother. "I was desperate."

The smug expression on his brother's face was expected. "Desperate and hopeful?"

That was his brother. "Desperate first," he said. "But then I once I realized what I'd done, I was hopeful."

"Why are you hopeful, exactly?"

Samuel tried to piece his feelings into coherent words. "I treated Leah horribly all those years ago. And I feel like it's important to apologize for what happened. I did her extremely wrong in a very public manner, Aaron. And this…seeing her at the expo and at the gallery last night? It has to mean something. All of this might be my only chance to do as much healing as she'll let me do. Fate, bashert…whatever it is, I'm being given a chance. I need to take it."

Aaron replied with a deep belly laugh that made Samuel feel three inches tall. "Are you kidding?"

"No." At least he thought he wasn't.

"You have to listen to yourself, brother of mine," Aaron

continued. "Because that's the funniest thing I've ever heard. This isn't a Yiddish drama or one of those HeartPix movies. You and Leah were a toxic high school disaster. Both of you should be over this by now. She's probably living her life, having processed this already, like an adult."

"The breakup and the reasons for the breakup *were* toxic," he replied, focusing on the word that stuck out like a sore thumb. "Not to mention, I haven't seen her since then. Until now. This…us coming back into each other's orbits, wasn't an accident, Aaron. And I didn't want to make it a missed opportunity."

"Interesting, but I disagree. The *whole thing* was a toxic disaster even though we didn't use those words back then. And you haven't seen her because you and she didn't *work* together as people. You were clinical. You're…flat; she's tough and so you ended up toxic."

His brother was usually a good judge of people and their personalities, but he'd never expected to hear Aaron talk about Leah in ways that made it clear he'd never understood her, which wasn't a discussion he wanted to have with Aaron, ever. Now he settled for the most important thing. "No matter what, we're now adults and I'd like to heal things because I have the chance."

"You know what I think?" Aaron asked.

"No," Samuel replied, knowing he was going to hear his brother's thoughts whether or not he wanted to.

"You're going backwards instead of forwards and not

focusing on the big picture. You're succeeding in business. Judith's ketubah is not bashert. Do your job. You're getting more commissions and you're getting more successful. Don't blow it."

Samuel nodded, but this situation with his life and with Leah was much more. And he had no desire to explain to Aaron some of the other intricacies that surrounded him and Leah, the things that seemed to be pulling them closer despite themselves.

But more importantly, it wasn't Aaron's assessment of the situation he had to focus on; it was Leah's and the email she'd sent him.

LEAH ADJUSTED HER blazer over her dress and stepped into her heels.

Armor.

Her makeup and hair were perfect. The papers she'd pulled together the night before—the ones that brought tangible proof of what she contributed to the agency—were organized in a binder.

Now she checked the time.

She was ready.

She left her office and headed to see Gabriel 'Call me Bruck' Brucker. He was the head of the agency, and had been her boss and mentor for a long time. He'd held the door open for her when she left to go to law school, smoothed the path when she'd come back. Now she was ready for the next step.

At 10 a.m. sharp, she knocked on the door of his office.

"Come in."

He sat relaxed behind his desk, smiling up at her. "Leah. Good morning."

"Good morning, Bruck," she said. "Thank you for agreeing to this meeting."

"Of course. We've known each other a long time." He paused and she met his eyes across the desk. "What's on your mind?"

Right to the point. She sat down on a chair in front of his desk, put the papers on her lap. "The future."

"I see," he said. "How's the women's sports angle going?"

"I'm enjoying it," she said with a smile. "Five years after I signed my first clients, they're thriving. The segment of the industry is giving so many female and female-presenting athletes ways to succeed, more than they ever have."

Gabriel smiled, tapping his pen against the ink-covered blotter. "Good. I'm glad to hear that. Is there anything I can do to help you?"

She nodded. "Yes," she said, preparing herself to say what she needed to. "I've demonstrated to you that I've been an asset to the agency, and I very much appreciate everything you've done for me."

"Why do I feel like I'm not going to like this thing

you're asking?"

"If you don't, I've given you the wrong impression," she said. "Because what I want is to give back. I want to help to use my name and connections to build the agency further."

"What are you asking for, Leah? Be very clear."

"My name on the stationery. I want partnership."

She watched the older man nod his head, glancing down at his blotter before looking back up at her.

"Interesting," he said. "And you've thought this through?"

"I have," she said, gesturing toward the papers. "This is what I bring to the table, a roster of men's and women's clients, dynamic potential. High-profile."

"I'm not going to lie to you," he said with a smile. "I'm glad you've asked me about this, because I've been thinking about it. But this is a pretty big decision. Being a name partner in an agency is life-altering. So this is what I want from you before we think about moving forward."

This was not a no. This was definitely not a no. But what was it?

"Okay?" she said, as if she needed to confirm her interest before he continued the conversation and told her the requirements. "What do you need?"

"Outline document. Pluses and minuses," he said ticking off the points on his fingers. "Things your current clients need, what you need to be able to provide them those things, leaving time for both old and new clients and your own breathing space. Because when you're a partner, work-life balance won't exist. So back to your office, pull it together by the end of day."

This was what he wanted?

Easy.

Leah had gone through all her paperwork before coming in for this meeting, so pulling this information together would be simple. "I'm on it," she said. And then she paused. He didn't have to make it that straightforward, but he had. "Thank you."

"You're welcome," he said. "But this isn't going to be a walk in the park. In fact..."

She looked up at him. "Yes?"

He was tapping a date on his calendar. "Are you busy on Thursday?"

Thursday. Everybody in the city knew what was on Thursday: Bruck's annual get-together. Some of the city's movers and shakers, gathering for a small cocktail party that he and his wife hosted at their townhouse in Manhattan. "No," she said, trying to hold herself together. Because there was only one right answer she could give. "I'm not."

"Good. I know you have a life, but you probably know my wife and I hold a small cocktail party every year: ten people. Some people, some clients, and their significant others. I'd like to see you and your significant other there this year."

"I'd love to," she said without thinking.

"Good. I hoped you'd be able to make it. You send me your personal email and I'll send you the details."

"Thank you," she said.

"You're welcome. Looking forward to the email."

And as she left the office, her excitement turned to trepidation. She needed a significant other to bring to that party. Which reminded her of the crazy idea she'd had last night while watching the drama.

Because she had a call with Samuel at five.

He owed her.

Which meant she was about to suggest the most ridiculous thing she could think of and ask the '*hot sofer*' if he wanted to make them a dating contract.

AT 5 P.M., Samuel dialed the number Leah had given him. He had no expectations and had spent the better part of the day trying to remind himself of that.

Except when Leah answered the call, she didn't greet him with 'hello' or 'how are you?' What she did say was: "I need your help."

Which was great. "I actually need your help as well," he said, "but what do you need me for?"

"I need the presence of a boyfriend without actually having one. So I need to fake-date you."

"So," he ventured, once he tamped the fireworks of his

emotions down. "You're asking me because I pulled you into the wild situation at the expo?"

"Partially. This is a way to fix the mess we made with this whole thing in my family. But also I need to bring a significant other to a work function."

"What kind of work function?"

"Are you familiar with Gabe Brucker's annual cocktail party?"

She said it like he was supposed to know what it was. He didn't. "No," he said. "Sorry."

"It's a cocktail party, thrown by my boss and his wife at their townhouse. He's been throwing it for years, and this is the first time he's invited me."

"Nice." And then he paused, remembering something she'd said either at the expo or at the gallery on Sunday. "You're a sports agent, right?"

She paused. "Yes," she said. "I am. Hockey if you're curious, men's and women's."

"So you did what you meant to. Congratulations."

"I'm not sure why you're telling me this now," she said after a while where he wondered whether she was going to respond at all, "but sure. We don't need any emotional trips down memory lane. This whole thing is...professional. What did you need?"

"Significant other at a work function," he said, speaking quickly so that he didn't lose her, "maybe crowd control at comic con. But also..."

"We need to get this in writing," she said, cutting him off at the pass. "Equal in terms of events. Code of conduct. Expectations."

"How we deal with our families?"

"Yes," she said, as if he'd somehow come up with something surprising. "Families. Professional obligations and contracts."

"Speaking of contracts," he said in an attempt to change the subject, "have you heard of the Unicorns? It's a girls learn to play hockey program out of Westchester."

There was a long pause and he wondered what was going on. "Leah?"

"I have," she finally said. "What's going on?"

"My mentor—he's hired me to do letters for a logo for something to do with the program. And you work with women's hockey, which means you probably know about girls' programs, so I figured I'd ask."

"Let's talk about that more this week," she said. "What do you need to put together a contract?"

He could say a lot, try to get all the information over the phone like what she seemed to be aiming for, but that wasn't the point of this. At least for him. The point was to spend time with her, learn who she was now. And maybe try and get her forgiveness. "How about we hammer out the specifics of the contract in person?"

"Don't you need private space to write?"

He laughed. Privacy was important, but she was actually

asking him to make them something. It would be something that required her input and his in a way that would not only shape the document itself, but also the form it would take. Which meant nothing he would be doing could would be private. "We have to talk specifics, because this isn't a ketubah." He paused, giving himself a second to think. "Can you come to my apartment this week?"

"Don't you have a space in the city you work at? I don't want to have to trek all the way out to…"

"Queens. Where do you live?"

"Manhattan."

He snickered. "Still call it the city, hm?"

The sound of her answering laugh melted his insides. "You can take the girl out of Briarwood but can't take years of living in Briarwood out of the girl."

"Right. So, Queens?"

She paused. "Fine. I have a late day tomorrow. I'll come to Queens."

"Urgency?

"Yeah." She paused and he wondered if she'd finished talking. "Party's Thursday."

This was urgent. Right. No wonder why she was agreeing to come to his apartment. "So I'll see you tomorrow and I'll be your boyfriend on Thursday."

And when she hung up, he wasn't sure what to do with himself, or more importantly, how to calm his racing heart.

She was coming.

They were doing this.

Chapter Six

LEAH HAD PREPARED for this meeting as if she was negotiating with a professional team on behalf of a client. List of needs, some basic information and direction of her armor.

And breakfast.

Which was the result of a quick text sent this morning.

You have coffee? I'll bring bagels.

He didn't take that long to respond, thankfully, so she still had enough time to stop off at Baums—the rideshare car arriving just in time for her to make a detour for bagels she didn't want to take on the subway.

Even luckier for her, there was little traffic; the ride was fast and she could still smell the bagels when she got out onto the street in Queens. More importantly, Samuel's building wasn't the artist's special she expected. The building's large doors opened to reveal a smiling doorman who directed her to an elevator; the door creaked when she opened it, but the ride up to his floor was smooth.

Her shoes smacked against the tile floor as she headed down the hall to his apartment, which was all the way at the end of the hall; a small mat and a visible mezuzah the signs someone lived there. She hit the buzzer, knowing this was the point of no return.

"Thanks for coming," he said as he opened the door, looking adorable in ways he shouldn't. "I appreciate it."

"Can't stay for too long," she replied, grounding herself in the certainty of her departure. And the scent of what had to be coffee.

"Come in?"

The sound of his voice wrapped around her and she fought against it. But not too hard. For now, for this moment, he wasn't her enemy.

Yet.

But all she could manage was: "The bagels are getting cold."

He put his hand out in front of her face, as if he was trying to show her something. What it actually did was yank her back to reality, and as she crossed over the threshold, she was reminded that there was no turning back.

AS LEAH STEPPED inside his apartment, Samuel felt as if he were upside down. "Do you have any questions?" he asked, deciding to just go with it.

"What's this?"

She was pointing to a frame he'd stuck on his mantel; inside was a simple drawing. White blossoms on snow, encircled by braided branches. "A frame," he said. "An untold story."

She looked up at him as if he'd lost his mind. "What?"

He sighed, crossed the room to stand by her and took the frame off the mantel. "You know the blank space, in the middle," he said, pointing to it.

"I see it."

"That's where the ketubah goes. The text," he clarified. "I mean."

"So why did you call it an untold story?"

"Because it is," he said as he tried to figure out how to explain this to her without talking down to her. "Someone's going to turn this into the frame that holds the story of their lives. Now, it's just empty space. Not a ketubah, just a frame."

There was a pause as he watched realization dawn on her face, her eyes focused. "An open playing field. Victory after crossing through the brambles and thorns."

He looked closer; he hadn't really thought about more than just the drawing; it never helped when he went into a ketubah session with an interpretation of his own after all, and this frame was eventually going to be a ketubah. But he didn't tell her that. What he said was: "I could see that."

She nodded, and so he took it as an invitation to continue interpreting with her. "Couple had bumpy moments in the past, figured them out and entered into this blank space where they had the freedom to choose their path, whatever that is."

"Don't say it."

Her tone held a note of reprimand and he wasn't sure where it came from. "What?"

"You need a better poker face. Because that isn't us." She pointed to the frame. "Going through the brambles requires emotional work I don't have time for, and I'd imagine with everything going on—as a sofer and angling toward more comics work and all of the publicity you're getting, you don't have that kind of time either."

He wanted to tell her that he had all the time in the world, but telling her that now, even as she'd just arrived, and was still holding the bagels she'd brought, was a horrible idea. Instead, he reached for the bagels and turned toward her. "How did you get into agenting?"

"What is this?" she said with a laugh that didn't ring true. "Twenty questions? Then again, these are things you…we're going to need to know for the contract, and the party tomorrow night."

"Right," he said, the words pulling him back down to earth, which meant he crossed the room into the kitchen, grabbed a knife and his cutting board. "Why contract though?"

Risky question with a knife in his hand to be sure, but he figured he'd ask it as she headed toward the coffee maker.

"Protection," she began, removing the pot from the coffee maker and sounding as if she'd pre-rehearsed a speech. "Making sure we know what's expected of us and for how long."

He nodded, smelling the coffee as she poured herself a cup. "Is this going to have an expiration date or?"

"It'll last as long as our list of appearances does, I guess," she said, as if she needed to tick the mental boxes off the check list before opening her mouth. "I need a significant other to bring to tomorrow's cocktail party."

"Right. And I need to bring someone—" he wasn't going to be specific and tell her his mentor had actually asked for her "—to a party my mentor is throwing. And I have both a comic con signing and a crowd control problem."

"And you asked me about the Unicorns for info purposes, which means I can get you to a have a way of getting you first-hand knowledge and soft-launching you with my family."

"How?"

"One of my clients is one of the founders, and my niece is taking part this year. So you'll come to her trial practice."

"Right." This was dizzying. Suddenly there were events and a soft launch of their relationship?

Wow.

But he had to be neutral. "That's four. Anything else?"

"Maybe we do Shabbat? One and one, making it an even six?"

"Six events—an option to renew?"

She looked at him, surprised. "I don't know why we'd renew it."

"If things go well," he said, trying to be neutral, trying to keep calm. "I mean if we end up with more events, if we like how it's going…"

"If it goes well, you and I are going to have less time," she pointed out.

"Right," he said, grabbing for something. "But ending this is going to take us really close to the wedding, and if we're doing Shabbat at the end, there's going to be talk."

There was a long pause and he could see the moment she capitulated. "Fine. Option to renew."

A victory, small as it was, but he'd take it.

"Do we need anything else?"

He laughed. "I don't know. I've never done this before."

"Neither have I," she said. "I mean…no. I've read about it, watched movies about it, all of which show the agreement failing because the two people who fake-date don't know each other."

This was interesting. "So you think this will succeed for us because…we do know each other?"

She nodded, sure of herself. "We know each other enough to know how much of a bad idea we are."

We know each other enough.

Right.

He was going to have his work cut out for himself if his goal was to fix things. But as he tried to process the information she was giving him, all he said was "Okay. What about…physical contact?"

She blinked. "What do you mean?"

In that blink was a lot: anger, surprise. Shock. Did she think he was taking advantage of her? "I'm not getting that deep—don't worry about it," he said, trying to pull himself together.

"So explain yourself. Quickly."

He nodded. "Right. Here's the thing. We're going to be in public, doing public things. Events with business contacts and with family who need to believe we're doing this for real, right?"

The sword had been at least holstered, which was a good thing. "Okay?"

He continued. "We have to be clear about things between ourselves and vis-à-vis the outside world."

"Keep talking. What do you mean?"

"Nobody is going to believe we're doing this for real if you look at me as if you have an allergy to some specific part of my composition."

"Not every couple that fake-dates discusses…touching."

Did she study? Do research? Watch every single…piece of media that dealt with fake dating in some way? Did she read every book ever published that dealt with a dating agreement?

And then he remembered back to the earlier thread of their conversation. "You know we're not like those couples."

"How?"

Whether she hadn't anticipated this part of the conversation or she'd forgotten she'd given him the tools to discuss it, he didn't know. He forged ahead anyway. "We know each other. We have a history you don't want to get into. Which means that we know each other well enough to talk consent, and other things so that you don't act surprised when I touch you, or I glare at you when you touch me."

"Okay," she said. He was relieved; she was taking this seriously. Not treating it like some ridiculous attempt to get closer to her. The idea of making things clearer between them was his goal.

"So," she said. "What do you mean?"

He started with the basics. "Hands touching are okay?"

He waited; he could explain more, but that had to be up to her.

"Yes. We can hold hands in public."

He nodded, mentally going to the next places his hand would naturally want or be expected to go on her body if they were dating. "Put my arm around you, you put your arm around me?"

She nodded. "That works."

And then he took the next step, wondering how she'd react.

"And kissing?"

LEAH WAS ABOUT to lose her mind. Talking to Samuel, negotiating with him even, was a whirlwind of emotion and just...

She tried to pull herself together, focusing on the scratching of his pen on the paper. "Kissing?"

He nodded. "Yes. It might come up, it might...I don't know. I want to be prepared and I want you to be prepared."

Prepared. Right. Nothing would or could prepare her for what kissing Samuel would do to her emotionally. And even thinking about it made her take a long drink of the closest liquid available. Thankfully it was water. "Even though I think it's a horrible idea, we need to have kissing in the contract. We need to...prepare each other though."

He raised an eyebrow; if he'd said no, she'd have left or done something. But he didn't. He was quizzical, curious, not dismissive. "You mean some kind of signal that we're going to kiss?"

She nodded. "You were always a good kisser. That way leads to trouble if we're not prepared."

"Keeping our heads out of it, you mean?"

Glad he was on the same page, or at least didn't dismiss her out of hand, she said, "Exactly."

But this time he didn't just take her words in; this time he seemed to think about them as he took a bite of a bagel. "Maybe we should work through it? Work up to it?"

She nodded, steeled herself. Shoved the suddenly appearing emotions down deep inside. "Yes. We should."

Leah held her breath and reached for the hand he offered, grasping his fingers through the spaces he left her. It wasn't that hard, she reminded herself.

She felt the calluses, which he'd built from hours of time

spent at his craft, massaging her palms. She could wrap herself in the peaks and valleys of his hands, forget they were touching and just exist like that indefinitely.

"How are you?"

"I'm okay," she managed.

But even he could tell she was lying. Because when she let his hand go, she flexed and then loosened her fingers, as if she was trying to slow down her pulse and her emotions.

This was dangerous.

"We're done for the day?"

"We haven't discussed the consideration," she said, annoyed that she knew way too much about the law to neglect that when all she wanted to do was leave. "What I mean is we need to talk about what you're going to want me to give you, you know, in exchange for this whole thing?"

"How about something easy?"

"What do *you* mean easy?" Because many different people had many different interpretations of easy. She didn't know his. Not yet. And it could be the furthest thing from easy.

"One favor to be named later that is within your power to grant."

Something that was within her power to grant was fine; it wasn't her choice for the thing she was bargaining this contract with, but she'd take it. She needed this too much. "Okay," she said. "Yes."

Which meant the deal was done in all but the writing.

SAMUEL WAS EXHAUSTED and grabbed a bagel. As he took a bite, he realized that she'd run their conversation as tightly as a meeting, taking refuge in procedure when things got too emotionally hard. It wasn't a fight, wasn't combat, and yet…

Because the agenda he'd put together was there, laid bare by the end of hers. He swallowed. "Do you have time?"

"I should probably go," she said. "You can draw it up from what we talked about and my notes?"

The notes. Of course. The rather large red binder that now sat on his kitchen counter. "Probably," he said. "And if I have any questions I should…"

"Email," she said, the word flying as she reached for her bag.

"If you want me to draw it up, you know, you have to sign it."

"I do," she said, probably knowing he was grasping for straws. "And we have to walk into my boss's apartment together."

"That we do, right."

"So," she continued as if he hadn't said anything or at least stated anything that made an impact, "you'll email me when you've finished and if you have any questions."

"And you'll email me as soon as you have the information. Maybe we can sign just before we go?"

She nodded. "I can do that."

"But of course, feel free to contact me if you want to share your favorite gefilte fish defenses."

He waited for her reaction; they'd bonded over a shared love of gefilte fish as kids in Sunday school.

"You only need one," she said, her eyes sparkling in ways that warmed his toes. "Horseradish delivery vehicle. Why do people hate on the joy of gefilte when there are other fishy things in other cultures?"

He nodded. "Like kamaboko, those Japanese fish cakes with the pink outsides?"

"Those are good," she said. "I love them. But why not gefilte?"

"I mean," he said with a laugh. "So many reasons why not. But I'll settle for the texture problem."

"Kamaboko is gelatinous," she said. "Gefilte is like…what's that thing…I don't know. What do they call it? It's breaded or fried on the outside and has fish on the inside?"

He snorted. "You mean a fish cake? How can you compare gefilte to a *fish cake*?"

"Gefilte is like the raw bar of *fish cake*, or like *fish cake tartare.*"

"Why would you eat a *fish cake* if it wasn't fully cooked, or like smashed to oblivion and artfully arranged like tartare anyway?"

"Because people make all sorts of reasons to avoid gefilte or think it's weird. But then eat a whole bunch of stuff that's just as weird and say it's more special or more relatable than gefilte depending on the context." She shook her head and he could see the transformation in her. "Speaking of the context, I have to go. Leaving the bagels with you. Keep me posted, 'kay?"

He nodded, stood up and escorted her to the door. "I can do that."

And for just a moment he wanted to close the space between them.

But he didn't.

Instead, he let her go, let her leave. He had time.

All the time in the world to take them through the bumps and brambles and kiss her for real.

Chapter Seven

SAMUEL'S MIND WAS running all over the place. He'd thrown a bunch of deadlines into turmoil because he needed to finish their ketubah in one shot; it was a process. And by the time he was done, he was running short on time.

Which was, of course, when she texted him with the time he was supposed to meet her to head over to the cocktail party.

In the city? he'd replied.

Which was the weirdest thing to say. But she texted back.

If you can meet me by my office, that's fine.

If I can't?

Do you have a space you work in at the city? I mean in Manhattan.

He snorted before texting back; it had taken a few responses for her to pause and think about what she'd been typing. *I know what you mean. Stop explaining. My brother's office is in Manhattan. He rents a space. Where's your office?*

East side, 60th. Your brother's?

Downtown. Which might be easier for us because you have to sign the contract.

There was a long pause as the dots danced in front of his

eyes; once again he debated telling her that the conversation would be better served over the phone. Although in all fairness, he wasn't sure what she was using their conversation to avoid. Finally the dots stopped and her message popped up.

Let me get the address and I'll see if that makes sense.

He nodded. *That sounds good*, he typed before turning back to the flashing cursor on his computer screen.

Luckily for him, that was when his phone buzzed with an incoming text.

It's going to be a mess, but I guess we have no choice. Send me the address and I'll see you at 6:30. We'll go from there.

Sounds good. I'll be the one in the clown suit.

The dots danced in front of his eyes, and he could almost see the ire in them. Of course that was probably the product of sitting too long, staring at a computer or his list of projects.

If I didn't know you better, I'd throw the phone through the window. Casual, business casual, please. And socks. Despite way too many 'fashion experts' who proclaim socks are a bad idea.

He grinned. Got a bit of a rise out of her, probably too much. But she knew him and knew he'd never ever do that. Which was the point, making her remember their shared history slowly and easily so that she'd be ready to discuss their past. Once that happened, they'd discuss whether or not it was something they could overcome.

But he was getting ahead of himself, trying to plan beyond where they stood. All he needed to do was prep himself for an event and hope to whatever being in the world was in charge that he didn't look ridiculous. Or act in any way that embarrassed Leah.

Because then he'd lose what he really wanted from all of this, the thing that he was hiding behind some kind of favor to be named later, to ask from her.

An honest, true, real second chance.

LEAH HAD ABSOLUTELY no idea how she was going to survive the evening, but she'd made her choice. She wore a dress she'd been saving, a green halter dress that landed just below her knee. It was a perfect match with a pair of strappy heeled sandals and a bag with a gorgeous bit of green across the top.

Pretty. Put-together and professional.

A quick refresh on her makeup in the bathroom, hanging the garment bag on the back door of her office, quick fluff of her hair and then out the door to sign what she was calling 'The Dating Contract' at Samuel's brother's office space before heading up to the party.

So many things were running through her head, but when Samuel opened the door to his brother's office, her brain stopped.

Wow.

He wore charcoal gray suit pants that highlighted his waist, and a shirt rolled up to showcase his forearms; they even made the traces of ink on his hands look good.

And the color.

Green.

It matched her dress.

Which made her feel things she wasn't ready to discuss. Instead she glanced at her phone. "We're running a little tight, so if you..."

He nodded, took the contract she'd committed herself to out of a manila folder, and placed it on the table.

"Oh," she managed. Because it was gorgeous. Bold colors, red and blue, the center ice of the rink she spent the most time at, covered in microcalligraphy, blank lines at the hashmarks of the ice.

"You don't...like it?"

Far from it. So far from it that if they weren't running late already, she would have leaned across the table, erasing the space between them, and kissed him. "It's gorgeous," she said instead. "I really, really like it."

She also liked the shy smile that spread across his face.

"Really?"

She nodded. He was a star on the verge and he didn't believe it, which was something she valued after years of representing athletes who acted like the world revolved around them because they could shoot a puck. "You're good," she said. "You're really good at what you do. You're ridiculously talented."

"I know you don't like talking about things, but I will

say that it means a lot coming from you."

She didn't know what had come over her, but she couldn't help herself. "You're welcome."

Just this once, she closed the space between them, let him lean toward her, and kissed him. Kissed him for knowing her, kissed him for making the contract and kissed him for reasons she didn't want to acknowledge.

When he broke the kiss, she found herself breathless.

"This was…a bad idea or a good idea?"

"It was my idea," she said, "and I don't even know the answer to the question, but I'll tell you that I don't regret it."

"I don't either. Does it change anything?"

She shook her head, even as her thoughts were spinning wildly out of control. "No. It doesn't. Is there somewhere I can sign?"

He pointed to the long black line at the bottom of the parchment. "Usually we'd need witnesses, but people knowing is the last thing we want at this point, right?"

"Right," she said, still debating whether she needed to tell Naomi what was going on. But this wasn't the time; they had things to do. So instead of asking him anything else, she took the pen and signed the contract. And then she capped it before passing it his way.

She watched the muscles of his forearms move as he signed and dated it, making them, and it, official.

Operation 'Fake Dating the Hot Sofer' was a go. She didn't know if she'd survive it, but she had no choice at this point; she'd signed the contract and made the commitments.

"So," he said, swallowing, breaking her concentration, probably for the best.

She could see the flush run across his face, and she didn't want to hear him try to explain its origin beyond the fact that it was starting to get hot and humid outside. "Is there anything I need to know about tonight, other than you're being observed for a partnership or something…?"

"Don't say it," she said. "Please. Just…be. My boss, Gabriel Brucker—call him Bruck or Gabe, he'll tell you which, and his wife will be hosting, so any discussion about partnerships or anything of that matter, are strictly forbidden."

He nodded.

The relief that settled down on her shoulders was immeasurable. "And be careful of his wife."

"Why?"

And that was a long story if anything. How could she explain to someone who wasn't familiar with the situation? "Because every time she meets someone, she tests them. Deliberately and especially. I'm not sure what she thinks of me, so she might express…ideas."

He raised an eyebrow. "Like what kind of ideas?"

"The sorts of ideas possessed by a fifties housewife," she said, not even trying to disguise the snort. "Sorry."

"It's fine," he said. "I get it. Okay. So I'm acting calm, not pushing back and not pissing off anybody with my ridiculous belief about how people of any gender should be allowed to pursue the career path they want?"

She couldn't help the laugh that came out of her. "Be careful, because people might get ideas, and start thinking they have options, and that's never good. And it matters because my boss pays attention to her opinion about people, and she's testing me because he is."

He paused and she wondered what was going through his head.

"Okay. I get it. Genuinely on my best behavior with this person."

"Good," she said. "Thank you."

He nodded, and reached out, presumably to take her hand. And because this was a contracted event, because they weren't actually doing this, but also because she was nervous, she took it. His fingers were warm as they wrapped around hers, the peaks and valleys of his skin were familiar.

"We're doing this," he said as he squeezed her hand.

The gesture pulled her back to reality. She nodded, leading him onto the street and toward the subway line they needed. "Yep," she said. "We're doing this."

And as the doors to the subway closed behind them, she held her breath.

Chapter Eight

Event One: Cocktail party, home of Gabe Brucker

Purpose: Public networking for Leah

Samuel noticed that Leah held his hand throughout the subway ride uptown, and didn't let it go as they got off the subway, though she would probably argue that it was just because she didn't want him to get lost.

He didn't ask her if she was nervous; he knew, as sure as first the sunset of a June evening that she was. And not just because he could feel the sweat in her palms.

The fact she'd reached for his hand said more than any word she'd ever allow herself to say.

"It's just up here," she said quietly, as if she knew she was breaking the silence. She wasn't looking at him, but he didn't expect her to. She was navigating after all.

And then she stopped almost suddenly, dropping his hand to smooth her dress.

"Any last-minute words of advice?" he asked, hoping to break what felt like the rising, thick tension by pulling her back to where she seemed most comfortable.

"Don't screw it up."

Which he could have scripted, but all the same he nodded and took her hand back as they headed up the stairs.

The silence was impossible as they walked the stone steps of the townhouse, and instead of letting himself get lost in scenarios that he didn't know would happen, he wondered if she'd planned to match him.

Regardless, the color of her dress was mesmerizing and calming, which was the best kind of distraction.

At least until they arrived at the top of the stairs and the sound of the door opening altered his focus. An older man with salt and pepper hair and brown eyes stood there smiling. "Welcome," he said. "Come on in, Leah. And…"

"This is Samuel," she said.

"Samuel Levine," he said, offering his hand. The older man took it. "Nice to meet you, sir."

"Glad you could make it," the older man said. "I'm Gabriel Brucker, call me Bruck, and this is my home. Come on in, the both of you."

He followed Leah and Bruck into the house; it wasn't a big crowd, probably about as big as the art show he'd gone to with Liam. But yet each of them were professional contacts of Leah and their partners.

And she was stunning.

Absolutely stunning.

He could see the looks in the eyes of a few of the people as she walked in with him, the way she moved in and out of the group, smiling and just…

"She's a diamond," an older woman said, smiling. "You should hold on to her."

He nodded. "She is."

"Josephine Brucker," the woman said. "Gabriel's wife."

"Samuel Levine," he said, as politely as possible, knowing Leah's professional career depended on it. "Leah Nachman's boyfriend."

A brief nod, as he followed Josephine Brucker's gaze toward a crowd. It was as if Leah was holding court amidst a bunch of people.

God she was sexy.

"You seem to be okay with someone like her, someone who's so driven and so strong."

He smiled back at this woman, whose view of Leah and her relationships and her chosen career shouldn't matter…except it did. "She wouldn't be the Leah I love," he said choosing to answer Josephine Brucker's stereotypical views with naked, emotional honesty, "if she wasn't strong or driven. Women like Leah are rare gems, and I'd be a fool if I didn't recognize that."

Josephine Brucker looked him up and down, making him feel like he'd been put under an x-ray machine; thankfully Leah had briefed him in advance. He could see in the cast of Josephine Brucker's features that she was simply the product of another age, one where she'd been expected to…be something or someone else in order to make someone happy. That, or she'd had her own ambitions or aspiration chopped back by someone she thought understood her the way she deserved.

And yet all the same, once again, he had to remind himself that Leah's professional future hinged on the outcome of the conversation, and he wanted to say something; he would have, except he could tell that nothing else he said would matter.

Until Josephine Brucker turned back toward him and slowly but surely smiled. "Just be careful," she said. "A woman like that won't change her spots once you're ready to settle down."

What he wanted to say was that he didn't want to see Leah in stripes but he settled for something that made more sense. "The spots she has," he said, "fit her perfectly. Fit me perfectly. Fit us perfectly."

And the wild thing was that he meant it more than he'd ever meant anything in his life, so much that he wished the relationship was real, that they were real.

But instead of nodding at him, this time, clearly having made her judgment, she looked at him in a way that made him feel she wanted to pat him on his head. "That's nice, dear," she said as she walked away.

He wondered if he'd made the wrong decision, but he'd already decided that his penance for the things he'd done in the past was to never let that mistake happen again, to stand up for Leah while contracted to be in a relationship with her, or not, even when she couldn't hear it.

LEAH HAD BEEN deep in conversation with one of Bruck's longtime friends when out of the corner of her eye, she saw Samuel talking to Bruck's wife.

She knew this was going to happen; she'd even briefed him on it, and yet all the same it made her sweat where she stood. She desperately wanted to go over, stop the conversation, stop the world, and yet she didn't. She couldn't. It would destroy him in front of Josephine and destroy her chances at the partnership she so desperately wanted.

Which meant she had to listen to the older man talk about the interesting things happening with the New York Gothams, as well as a documentary that was filming about the Oakland Elephants. She wasn't a baseball person, but the story was an easy focus and less about a sport she didn't pay attention to, and more about the story of the documentary itself.

"I'm going to go and check on my wife," he said with a smile. "She's in the corner, getting herself a drink. It was nice."

"Nice to meet you," she said as he walked away.

As she tried to figure out what she needed to do next, she saw Bruck's wife shake her head. Which was a victory in itself. Josephine Brucker's conversations with people usually ended with loud stinging reprimands that had aftereffects even years later.

Except Samuel had managed to thwart whatever malicious intentions the woman had expressed in a way that wouldn't permit her to explode like she usually did.

Leah wanted to cheer.

She headed toward the drinks table in search of a reason to cross the room and congratulate him. But as she grabbed a glass of ginger ale, out of the corner of her eye, she heard her name. "Leah? Leah Nachman."

She turned, only to see Jessica Weiss, captain of the US Women's Hockey team standing there, grinning.

Jess was represented by another agent, but the women's hockey world was small and they'd seen each other at different events because some of her clients were Jess's teammates both in the NAWHL and on the national level.

"Jess," she said. "This is a surprise."

"I'm arm candy tonight," she said with a laugh. "My name wasn't on the invitation, but I'm really glad I'm here."

Every once in a while, she'd forget that Jessica Weiss was dating the head of one of the biggest Jewish charities. "I'm glad to see you."

"I wanted to tell you about the gala," Jess said.

Leah blinked. There were tons of galas and ceremonies and awards that dotted the intersection between sports and charity. "Refresh my recollection?"

"Bruck has an invitation," Jess began. "But anyway, in a few weeks Evan and I are hosting a women in sports gala. And we're honoring the Unicorns."

"Oh that's amazing," she said. And then something clicked; the fact that Samuel had been asking for information about the Unicorns.

"It is. Evan's even pulling in a favor from his buddy who works at BP comics for the logo. It hasn't been done yet, but we're crashing everything so...we had basic invites and are revealing the logo as a sort of...draw for the donation part of the event."

And that made sense. So much sense.

This is why Samuel needed information about the logo, and why he was going with her to practice on Saturday. Yet another reason she needed to find him.

But none of this, none of the strings that were tying them in tangled ways together, was bashert.

AFTER FINISHING THE conversation with Josephine Brucker, Samuel found himself at loose ends, and debated going in search of Leah. Of course she was already in a conversation with someone else, someone he vaguely recognized. Instead, she went to get a glass of ginger ale on the other side of the room.

"Takes a lot to be in a relationship with a strong woman."

He blew out a breath, turning toward a gentleman wearing a blazer, a pair of black pants and oxfords. "If it's not as easy as breathing, you're with the wrong woman."

The gentleman he was talking to blinked, as if he hadn't expected to hear the statement the way Samuel said it, and as if there was a bit of awe, if not understanding. "Yes," the gentleman said. "It's hard for people who aren't with the right person. There are difficult moments for sure, but when the underlying conflict is that you want them to be a different person, you're in the wrong relationship with the wrong person." He paused and extended his hand. "Evan Lefkowitz," he said. "My girlfriend's on the other side of the room."

And then it clicked. "My mentor is Liam Hernandez," he said. "I'm Samuel Levine."

"You're working on the logo, I hope!" Evan said with a grin.

"I am," Samuel said. "I'm really excited, testing out things."

"I'm so glad he convinced you to do this. It's nice to meet you."

"Great to meet you too," Samuel said, smiling. "It's nice to make the connection face to face."

"It is, right? I hope Liam hasn't said anything awful about me?"

Samuel laughed, the weight of making a good impression off of his shoulders. "Just things that make me think you're a kindred spirit—I also had a picking-grass phase instead of playing goalie when I was young."

Evan snorted making Samuel, once again, feel right at home. "He's never going to let that go. Ever. But that's why he's my friend, He's got a good eye though. Keep him close."

"I was lucky," Samuel replied. "Lucky that they assigned me to him after design school."

"He is the lucky one. Says my mezuzah and the ketubah I'm looking at, not seriously, of course."

And as they continued to talk, Samuel found himself relaxing even more, until Evan looked up and realized what time it was before heading to find his girlfriend, leaving Samuel with a parting 'see you at the gala. Can't wait to see the logo.'

Apparently, he had a great deal to tell Leah on the way home. This, he decided, was going to be interesting.

WHEN JESS LEFT to usher Evan out the door, Leah took it as her cue to go and find Samuel.

"Hey," he said.

She held his hand; she wasn't sure why she felt it was necessary, but she did it anyway. "You're amazing," he said as they headed down the stairs of the townhouse, and out into the summer night.

"I...don't know what happened?"

"You don't?"

She shook her head. "No. I don't."

"They love you," he said. "It felt like you were holding court, you know? Like everybody wanted to talk to you and everybody wanted to see what you were saying. You did amazing and I'm so glad you had me come with you."

"You slayed a dragon," she said as they stopped in front of a subway station. "Is this fine?" She gestured to the sign in front of the entrance showing which trains the station serviced. And in which directions.

He nodded. "This is the one I need to get back to Queens. Speaking of Queens, I was in awe of you tonight."

"You," she said, bringing the subject back to what was important, "were wonderful. And now I know why you're asking for information about the Unicorns."

He nodded. "Yep. I was...talking to Evan Lefkowitz tonight."

"Of course you were," she said with a laugh. "You know he doesn't talk to many people."

"He and my mentor are old friends," he replied. "So I had an in."

"Which was impressive." She paused, wondering what was happening. "Are you going to the gala?"

The sound of his laugh made her relax. "Yeah. I am. I think Evan wants me there, which is such a weird thing to say."

"You spend way too much time living in self-deprecation," she said. "Do you realize how talented you are?"

Unlike so many people she'd encountered, he shook his head. "I don't," he said. "And I think that's the best thing for me. I never want to stop growing, never want to take my work or the opportunities I'm given for granted."

If nothing else, that made her feel the thread that tied them together and actually admit, even to herself, that it existed. "So," she said, trying to pull herself back to reality. "That's why you have a crowd control problem." Thinking about what going to a comic convention when he was signing was going to be like almost terrified her. "You're so...genuine."

"I try," he said. "I... It's weird. Finding my place, taking advantage of my opportunities without overdoing it, and remembering why I'm there in the first place."

"Speaking of opportunities, I guess we're going to the gala?"

He nodded, faster than she would have liked but in a way that made her breathe, as if she'd been nervous about his answer.

Which made no sense. Then again, nothing made sense about her interactions with him.

Zero.

"I'd like that," he said. "I'm glad we can go together."

And that was it.

That was what made her want to kiss him. She could blame it on the night sky, but it was all her and her stupid...whatever that drew her closer to him, her hand reaching up to trace the path of his cheekbone.

"Would you like to kiss me?" he asked, his voice enveloping her like a cloud.

"Yes," she said, pulling him or the thread closer, reveling in the feel of his breath on her face in the middle of a Manhattan evening, his hands on her shoulders as she leaned into the kiss. She wanted to dive into him, wanted to lose herself in him.

And when she pulled back there was reality. There was the light of the subway entrance, the fact that morning was going to come quickly and she had to be ready for whatever was going to happen. "So…I'll see you Saturday?"

"Yeah. You'll text me the details?"

She nodded as they headed down the escalator, and through the gate where they slid their cards through. They stood on the train platform together; the local, not the express, going downtown, so he could switch to the train he needed after one stop, and she could take hers the rest of the way home.

As she watched him get off the train, she found that she didn't want him to leave, and was terrified to discover that the real problem was that she wanted to be with him, despite all of the complications of a fake relationship and their real history.

She was, in short, in trouble.

Chapter Nine

FRIDAY MORNING, SAMUEL had too many thoughts running around his head to consider staying and working in his apartment, so he headed to the subway, following the directions to Liam's new apartment.

He and Leah had kissed under the stars.

He'd call it something, but it was exciting, surprising and so much more than he'd ever expected.

Which was why he'd been lucky Liam had texted him.

"Come on in," Liam said when he arrived. "Oliver and I are playing with ideas. And you have been moving and shaking."

"I have?"

Liam nodded, gesturing to his phone. "You won't believe the text I got last night from a very giddy Evan Lefkowitz who wanted to congratulate me, for getting me to persuade you to agree to the logo, and for him to congratulate himself for meeting you."

"You met Evan Lefkowitz last night?" Oliver asked.

Samuel nodded. "I went to a party with my girlfriend."

"I was wondering about that girlfriend of yours," Oliver

said.

Samuel smiled, slowly getting over the fact that Oliver Goldsmith had gone from being an inspiration to a guy who was asking about his girlfriend.

The fake girlfriend he wanted to make real.

"Yeah," he managed. "It was nice to spend a night watching her shine at one of her professional events."

"He's not telling you the details," Liam said. "The party he's so casually referring to is that sports party…the sports agent who invites a select number of movers and shakers? So your girlfriend…"

"Is a sports agent," Samuel confirmed with more than a little pride. "And works with the guy who hosts the party. Bruck? I think."

"Yeah," Liam said. "That's the guy. Anyway, you're bringing this girl to the party I'm hosting for Oliver over here."

Samuel nodded. "I am. I'm also bringing her to Comic Con."

"You're doing Comic Con?" Oliver asked. "Very cool. Me too."

"Yeah. Signing posters for MoviePix."

"Soon you'll be signing other things," Oliver said, before giving Liam a look that made Samuel nervous.

"If I have my way," Liam said, breaking through the thoughts running through Samuel's head, and gesturing toward the kitchen table. "But we'll keep you posted. But for now, give me a few ideas in terms of letter design for this logo."

Letters. Logo. It was as if a light went off over his head. "Right. When do we need this by?"

"Why?"

"Because my girlfriend is getting me into a Unicorns practice this weekend."

"Excellent," Liam said. "Let's start working and we'll conference on Monday so we can get this done."

And as Samuel took out his pens and sat down next to Liam, he let himself prepare, and maybe get a little more excited, about what his future held.

LEAH WAS STILL slightly off kilter when she arrived at the office on Friday morning, but she was ready to tackle most everything that came her way.

As she sorted through her schedule, there was a knock at the door. "Come in," she managed before catching a glance at the individual who had requested entry.

Of course it was Bruck. Casual, shirt-sleeves folded up to his elbows, the hazards of white dress shirts in this part of the summer.

"Morning, Leah," he said.

"Bruck. Hi…I'm sorry…"

Bruck raised an eyebrow as he walked into the office.

"Why are you sorry?"

"I'm a bit of a scatterbrain this morning," she said with a laugh, gesturing at the papers strewn across her desk and the remnants of her coffee as it sat on the corner. "Trying to organize things at the moment. And it's a bit of a mess…"

Bruck shook his head, his eyes addressing her as if she'd lost her mind. But all the same, his finger pointed toward the door. "Can I?"

She nodded; even though the potential conversation subject put butterflies in her stomach. What could he want to talk about?

Had she done something?

Bruck reached around to close the door before he settled into a chair in front of her desk. "Your clients set your schedule," he said. "It is nice to see you in the office semi regularly, but when push comes to shove and your schedule is what it is, it's yours, not mine."

She nodded, not sure what to say. "Thank you?"

"The more pressing concern," Bruck continued, as if she hadn't said anything, "is that there's an event I'd like you to attend in my place."

She nodded. "Okay? Any particular reason?"

"I want to support this organization," he said. "And you're the best fit to attend, especially when I can't go."

She nodded, as the information sank in. "Oh?" she asked. "What organization is this and what kind of an event?"

"It was supposed to happen a few months ago, and a bunch of people were convinced it wasn't actually happening. But Tzedakah Exchange—Evan—specifically took over the event, overhauled the whole thing and are putting on a gala."

"Oh wait...Jessica Weiss and I were talking about this last night."

"Yes, I saw that you were talking to her." He smiled. "I have to tell you that my wife took a shine to your young man. She wants him to make a mezuzah for our house in the Hamptons, but that's another story."

Which was interesting because Josephine liked *nobody*. Not a soul.

And yet she liked Samuel.

She finished the conversation with Bruck, agreeing to attend the gala, this time not as Samuel's guest, but in Bruck's place.

And yet all she could think about was Samuel.

Which was going to be interesting.

WHEN HE GOT back from Liam's Friday afternoon, Samuel started to prep for the drive to Briarwood. Friday night dinner with his family was the priority and, after that, when he'd usually relax, the rest of the weekend was full. Saturday afternoon he'd go to the Unicorns practice with Leah, and then go back to the city for Sunday's comic con.

Thoughts of Leah made him wonder how she'd react when he saw her; what she thought of how he'd done at the cocktail party and what that meant for her career…

And the kiss.

But he couldn't let his mind drift toward any of those things because he needed to focus on packing. He was halfway through when his phone started to buzz.

He picked it up and realized that the person calling him was Leah.

"Hey," he said. "How are you?"

"Good. I wanted to let you know that not only did I get the official invitation for the gala, but also let you know that you impressed Josephine Brucker."

"Gala? Which…right." The information clicked and settled in his head. The logo and the conversation he'd had at the party. "That's amazing," he said. "And I'm glad. I was worried."

"You're much better at this fake boyfriend stuff than you thought," she said, her words hitting him hard.

Harder than he wanted them to.

Which was when he reminded himself he had time to convince her. So much time. "So," he said, as if to remind her, "we're going to the gala?"

"I guess we needed that extension?"

Vindication was great, he decided. But more importantly. "Tomorrow?"

"Four at the JCC, okay?"

He nodded. "Right. And then do you want a ride back to Manhattan?"

He waited, wondering what she'd say.

"You know what, yes. Which means I can take the train with my cousin tonight."

He nodded. "So see you tomorrow at four?"

"Tomorrow at four. Looking forward to it."

And when he ended the call, he was more excited than he'd been before.

LEAH WAS EXHAUSTED. Catching the train back to Briarwood was a pain, and finding two seats together during rush hour was a minor miracle. But she and Naomi managed it and were headed back to Briarwood. "So what's up?" she asked her cousin.

"Livvy's talking about a family trip but I noped out of that conversation so fast."

"Why?"

"Because I'd rather not waste my time planning something that is actually not going to happen."

Leah snorted. "Your parents would want a family trip this close to Judith's wedding?"

"And then there's the Livvy factor of it all," Naomi confirmed. "Like it's actually going to happen, knowing my sister is the worst workaholic in the world, which is saying something coming from me."

"I wasn't going to say anything," Leah said with a laugh.

"Which is good, because I was going to ask you for an update on the boyfriend situation."

Leah considered her cousin. This wasn't Naomi's style. If Naomi wanted to ask her something, she'd do it, not…like this. Which meant someone had asked Naomi for information. "Who's sniffing?" Leah asked.

Naomi gave a long sigh. "You're going to find out this weekend anyway, but Judith was sniffing around for info."

Of course she was. Why was she not surprised Judith was trying to get information? Judith was an incurable busybody when it came to the matters of Leah's life.

"But meanwhile, your sister-in-law is trying to keep everybody patient, but nobody knows impatience like Nachmans."

And suddenly, Leah had a brand-new respect for Shayna. "Which is wonderful," Leah replied, "because I'm taking him to Ramona's hockey practice on Saturday afternoon."

"Very interesting soft launch to the relationship." Naomi paused. "If that's what this is."

Leah raised an eyebrow. "Excuse me? I…"

Naomi shook her head as the train pulled into the station. "I'm the last person in the world who should be judging this or you," she said. "But you need to figure out what you want from this relationship, and what you're willing to give."

And as she pondered what she was going to do, Leah was even less sure of herself than she'd been before. But more importantly, she wondered how she was going to survive the weekend.

Chapter Ten

SAMUEL SPENT THE entire drive to Briarwood on edge; the weekend was going to be busy, not the usual ease of Shabbat at his parents' house.

And there was Leah, in the same town, probably having discussions over challah and wine with her family.

Yet the discussion at the table was easy, the conversation contrary to everything going on. Even more wonderful, the Union were playing baseball on a Friday night, which meant his father and brother-in-law were glued to the television.

"Can you stop yelling at the announcers?" Tommy asked from his usual perch next to his father-in-law. Samuel's father and brother-in-law could talk baseball in general, and the Union in specific, for hours.

Samuel himself was a casual fan, not as steeped in the analytics of the situation as either Tommy or his father. "They're clearly biased," he scoffed. "I can't help it."

"Maybe you can leave and help me instead?"

His mother stood just by the doorframe, smiling at the assembled crowd, Aaron having gone upstairs to organize some things the second dinner was over.

Annoyed that nobody else was getting up to help, and glad to lend a hand, Samuel turned to his mother and smiled. "Coming," he said, leaving Tommy to watch the game with Samuel's father, unencumbered by his opinions of the announcers who clearly favored the losing team, the ones not wearing the Union's pinstripes.

As they headed into the kitchen, his mother looked in his direction and shook her head.

"What?" he asked. "You have this look on your face."

"Well that's because you don't look good," she said once the door to the kitchen swung closed. "What's wrong?"

He blinked. "I'm fine," he said. "Really."

"I know my son," she said pausing to ruffle his hair.

He was in his thirties and his mother was ruffling his hair. He sighed, shook his head and smiled. "I'm fine."

"Is it your dating life?" she asked, as if she hadn't heard him speak. "Do you need me to set you up? I know nice people."

He sighed. This was the conversation he'd expected from his mother earlier in the day when he'd first arrived in Briarwood, telling her that he was going to have a busy weekend. "I'm fine, Ma, but you..." He trailed off and then pulled himself together. "You have a son who's happily married, Ma. What's going on? Why this now?"

"You mistake me," she said.

He nodded, gestured with his hand. "So tell me. Why this now?"

"I want *both* my sons *happy*," his mother said, before pressing the start buttons on the dishwasher and turning toward the coffee maker. "Married, single, with grandchildren, grandpets…doesn't matter."

He nodded. That was reasonable.

"And you?" His mother patted his shoulder before rolling up her sleeves. And wiping down the counter. "You are not happy."

"I'm fine, Ma," he repeated. "Really."

His mother shook her head. "I'm your mother. You cannot fool me."

"He's stressed, "Aaron said as he entered the room. Of course his brother would have something to say about commitments and stress. "He's overcommitting himself with no real plan because he's afraid."

"I'm enjoying myself," Samuel said, trying to explain what was going on to both his brother and his mother. "I'm finally at the stage of my career where I'm doing what I've always wanted, not just one thing…"

"You're getting noticed," Aaron said, as if he was explaining life to both him and his mother. As if Samuel didn't understand his own life or career. "Just don't enjoy it too much or you'll end up stuck in a place you don't want to be."

"I'm fine," he insisted again. "I'm finally figuring things out."

"See that you do," his mother said looking back and

forth between them. "Both of you need to go to your separate corners. Give each other a break. It's Shabbat."

In the brief silence, Samuel could hear Tommy and his father yelling happily at the television.

Yep. It was Shabbas.

Life, he decided, no matter how busy he was, was good.

Event Two: Unicorns hockey practice

Location: Briarwood, JCC, Briarwood New York

Purpose: Soft launch for the relationship in front of Leah's family/professional inspiration and networking for Samuel

Leah was excited.

Her niece, Ramona, had wanted one thing for her fourth birthday: hockey lessons. And considering that one of 'Auntie Leah's' clients was a founder of one of the most famous U-4 girls' hockey programs, Auntie Leah was able to deliver.

Which was why she stood in the parking lot, waiting for her sister-in-law.

Once they arrived, Ramona, her newly minted four-year-old niece raced over, her arms outstretched. "I get to play hockey."

"You do," Leah said squeezing her niece. "And it's okay to have fun and..."

"I'm going to play forever," the determined little girl insisted as they headed into the building.

"Thanks for this," Shayna said, hefting the bag that held Ramona's hockey things. "She hasn't been able to talk about anything else."

"It's the least I could do," Leah said. "I hope she likes being on the ice."

Shayna laughed. "Nate and Shim have been taking her skating to break the skates in for the past few weeks, and they haven't been able to get her *off* the ice. I suspect she's going to be in heaven."

"I am," Ramona said, a broad smile on her face. "Auntie Leah, I'm going to score a *goal* and wear a tutu."

Leah grinned at her niece. "You're going to score a goal in a tutu, huh?"

Ramona nodded, a serious expression on her face. "I'm going to wear a tiara and a tutu and score a goal."

Leah smiled. "You can do anything," she said.

Ramona beamed as she headed toward a group of girls chattering in the hall.

"Gotta go in there," Shayna said. "But I have to ask. What's up with Samuel?"

Leah sighed, but remembered what Naomi said. She owed Shayna. "We're exploring," she said. "We're exploring how dating feels after all these years."

Shayna raised an eyebrow. "Look," she said. "You will forgive me if I don't believe you. What I do believe, and won't push about, is that you seem happy. Whatever the hell is going on with the two of you, just promise me that you won't let the pressure get to you."

"Pressure?"

What the hell was Shayna talking about, pressure?

In response, Shayna adjusted the bag on her shoulder. "Judith has been sniffing out information like it's her job, and Naomi seems to be cagey. Which means she knows something. Everybody wants to know what's going on, not to mention you and Samuel are known to have a difficult history."

Difficult was putting it mildly, and it seemed Leah owed Shayna her firstborn. "I mean…"

"But anyway," Shayna interrupted. "All of that? What I just talked about? *That* is pressure—the stuff outside. But the stuff outside isn't what matters. What does is what sits between you two."

Which was true if she was talking about a normal couple and their normal relationship. But she and Samuel were complicated and, at the end of the day, Leah wondered if what sat between her and Samuel were a bunch of tangled threads and a contract. But she didn't want to tell her sister-in-law that. What she said was: "Okay?"

"Good." And then both she and Shayna heard Ramona's excited wail. "I think I've got to go."

As Leah watched her sister-in-law head into the dressing room with her niece and the huge bag of equipment, she heard the alarm on her watch go off.

Samuel was going to arrive soon.

And she wasn't sure what to make of it.

ON SATURDAY AFTERNOON, Samuel found himself getting out of his car, on the passenger side, at the JCC. His plans, including driving Leah back to the city, had gone out the window when his brother's car needed to go to the shop.

"Thanks for letting me borrow the car," Aaron said with a laugh.

"Not a problem," Samuel said. He was looking forward to what was going on inside, after all. "Keep me posted on where you are, and I'll let you know when I'm done."

"I will," Aaron said. "No sure what our plan is, but I'll keep you posted."

Which was Aaron's way of saying 'don't wait up.'

Which made sense; Aaron and Tommy had plans for the day, which was why Aaron had said comic con wasn't an option. And transport wouldn't be a problem; mass transit and rideshare existed.

And as he headed into the rink, he bumped into someone. "I'm sorry," he said.

Until he realized he'd run into Bryce Emerson. Bryce Emerson was many things: a sculptor, a painter, a multimedia artist who became famous when his art had been featured in a music video. Now he made goalie masks and silly T-shirts and sculptures that fetched a great deal of money at auction.

And Bryce was standing in front of him at the JCC.

"You're Samuel Levine?"

He picked up his jaw from the floor. "I am. I've been following your career," he said, the words flying out of his mouth faster than he could catch them. "You might say I'm a bit of a fan. I like how you work in different mediums…"

"Like recognizes like," Bryce replied, much to Samuel's amazement. "The jewel of it all is how similar the things you style are." He paused. "When my wife asked what mezuzah we wanted, I said I wanted the scroll to be one of yours."

This was…beyond words. He'd eventually have to thank his brother for instituting a business model that separated him from the names of his clients. No wonder his brother had an inflated opinion of his business prowess.

Because now, he was standing in front of an artist he admired…who was telling him he was not just a fan but owned something he'd designed. "Wow," Samuel managed. "You're kidding me."

"Not kidding. Not at all. In fact, do you think we can talk about possibly making something together?"

Without a pause he nodded. "Yes," he said, trying to keep from losing his mind. "I'd love to see what it would look like to have my…style of calligraphy on a mask or…whatever."

"When you go to watch a four-year-old girls' hockey practice," Bryce said with a laugh, "interesting things happen. Why are you here?"

"My girlfriend," he said without thought. "Her niece is doing the practice, and I'm doing a logo for a ceremony..."

"Hold on," Bryce said. "You're dating my wife's agent?"

"Your wife is represented by Leah Nachman?"

Bryce nodded again, and Samuel felt the bunch of strings that tied him to Leah tighten. "My wife, Carly, *is* repped by Leah. So you're dating Leah, hm?"

He nodded, letting the words sink in. "I...am," he said. "We're figuring things out."

"Good to hear. She's a good person. And she's been good for my wife. And you're doing the logo for the Tzedakah Exchange gala?"

"With my mentor, yes. I'm going to get some ideas about the energy for the logo, you know?"

"I do. I really respect that." Which felt fantastic to hear from Bryce, someone whose career *he* respected. "How about this? We have a design session out at my place in Rivertown on Monday? Bring your mentor and whoever else he has working on the logo."

Which was a wonderful invitation, except he felt strange accepting on Liam and Oliver's behalf. "I'll talk to them. I'm actually seeing them at comic con."

"Oh wow," Bryce said, and the awe in his voice made Samuel feel strange in a way he couldn't quantify. "Comic con. Anyway, let's go watch the practice and we'll touch base later."

And as he and Bryce headed toward the rink, yet again, Samuel found himself thinking about the twists and turns his life had taken. And that he was enjoying every minute.

LEAH WAS SITTING on a metal bench in June. It was cold, which meant she had a cardigan. On the other side of the glass were a group of young kids, including her four-year-old niece. They were skating along, wearing tutus, and learning how to skate around cones.

The cones, however, were larger than the usual cones used in these sorts of hockey drills, covered in sparkles and had one distinct horn, because the skaters had been charged with avoiding harming the 'unicones' in their path.

"I've seen people talk about it," Leah admitted. "And I've seen a few practices, but this is absolutely wild to watch."

"The important part," Shayna said, a huge smile on her face, "is that she's having a blast."

And sure enough, Leah could see the twinkle in her four-year-old niece's eyes under the plastic shield of her helmet as she came around to try her luck to avoid harming the so-called 'unicones.'

Which was the best possible thing that could have happened. "I'm so glad," Leah said.

Carly, her client and one of the founders of the program, nodded, the pride obvious in her voice in a way that made Leah giddy. "I love how the program's succeeded over the years, and I love how people have come to enjoy it."

"It's such a great thing," Shayna said, as if confirming and affirming Carly's statement at the same time. "It introduces hockey and makes it available to girls of a younger generation than we would have otherwise."

But as Carly and Shayna started to discuss specifics of how to actually get Ramona set for the September start date to what would be her program, Leah found herself heading down to the side of the rink. There, the boards and the rails atop them gave her a place to lean and stand. Watching this practice was *fun.*

This was the first time in a while where she was watching a hockey practice because she *wanted* to. She wasn't watching for clients or prospects or potentials. She was watching her niece, like her nephew before her, play the sport for the very first time, and learn something she'd take time getting to know.

"They're wearing tutus."

She didn't have to move to realize that it was Samuel; she'd already established that she could recognize his voice anywhere. Now he sounded surprised, but the greater, deeper surprise was the fact he was there standing beside her, his arms folded on the rail. But instead of telling him to move his hands out of the way like a freaking nudgy nudnik, she nodded. "That they are."

"They're playing hockey wearing tutus?"

Once again, he sounded surprised, which meant she needed to nip that in the bud. "I told you they'd be wearing tutus," she said, trying not to roll her eyes. "What they're actually learning is how to handle a stick. The tutus are a value-added benefit."

"You did tell me. I wasn't sure how it would look is all," he said, holding his hands in her direction, palm out, as if he was a traffic guard. "They look like they're having fun, so it doesn't matter."

Satisfied she didn't need to lecture him, she nodded. "Exactly."

"What are those?"

She followed the direction of his fingers, toward a group of skaters who looked like they were wearing something strapped to their helmets.

She looked at it for a minute, and then realized what it was. "It looks like a unicorn horn," she said. "I think they're meant to help the kids get used to the feel of a helmet on their heads, and also help them find some balance."

His smile was easy. "Horn's the added benefit?"

"You catch on quick," she said with a laugh. "Innovative ways to teach some of the most basic fundamentals."

"I'd say this is innovative, but that's why they're winning this award, right?"

Leah shouldn't have been surprised at Samuel's insight,

but she was all the same. "Yes," she said. "Not all U-4 girls' hockey programs should look like this, but this one does. The girls who play on this program like the added elements. There are other programs, but this one is going to be right up my niece's alley."

"It's fascinating," he said. "Great to watch and the logo should be that gorgeous too."

She nodded. "These are little girls who…don't have to decide between hockey and tutus, between crowns and swords. They probably, like my niece, saw an older sibling play, got jealous and there they are."

"There they are," he said. "I like it. They look like they're having fun."

"I think they are," she said. "Are you?"

"I just got here, and I'm not going to, like, sugarcoat the fact that I like watching with you, and…"

"What else?"

"Bryce Emerson wants to collaborate with me. You represent his wife?"

Leah nodded, feeling the pull of those freaking pieces of string. But instead of saying that, she shoved it aside. "Interesting," she said instead. "But now, let's watch some little girls fall in love with hockey."

And she wasn't, under any circumstances, going to fall in love with him. Again.

Chapter Eleven

PRACTICE HAD BEEN wonderful. Samuel had really enjoyed watching the excited little girls get their first taste of hockey, including the little babysitting with someone who'd been introduced as Leah's client.

"What did you think?" Leah asked as they walked outside. There was expectancy in her eyes, as if she was looking for him to say something in particular.

"I can see letters dancing in my head," he said before stopping and realizing she didn't speak Samuel anymore. "I mean, it was amazing and inspiring and wonderful."

Leah nodded. "I'm glad it was what you were looking for."

"More than that," he said, concerned she was thinking this solely had been an assignment. "I mean…" He shook his head in order to try to keep himself from gushing. "I understood why the program was getting an award before. I really understand now."

"I'm glad," she said, and if that wasn't approval in her voice he'd eat his socks. He wanted her approval for many reasons, but more importantly, he wanted to make sure she knew he was a different person.

"Me too," he said.

She laughed and then paused. "Now what? I mean when do you have to be there tomorrow? When do you need to leave?"

He blinked, then realized he had to give her an important update. "Can you drive?"

"I thought you were going to," she said, "but I can."

"Something happened," he said, realizing he'd probably lost whatever point she'd given him. "I do owe you a ride back to the city or to Briarwood, but I can't do it today."

This time, her nod was of understanding; he still spoke Leah after all. "Okay. Do you need to get anything from your parents' house or are we good to go?"

He shook his head, pointing to his messenger bag. "I have everything. Whatever I don't have, either my brother can bring back when he comes to the city or I can get, or you know, buy."

"Okay then," she said as they headed to the car. And as she got in, organized herself in the driver's seat she looked at him in a way that knocked his socks off. "What's the story?"

"My brother," he said as he settled into the passenger seat of Leah's car. "He'd promised Tommy a nice weekend outing, only to be thwarted by his car."

Leah nodded as she pulled out onto the main street. "You couldn't stand in the way. Okay."

He smiled back at her. "Thanks. I appreciate it."

"Not a problem."

And as she pulled onto the highway that would take them back to the city, Leah rolled the windows down and turned up the music.

The song was…a cover, he was sure. The guitars were softer in the original, but the fun, pop punk cover suited them and their mood, and the road seemed to obey their whims; the highway was open, not as many cars as he'd expect on a Saturday night.

The irony, of course, was that the song was about a guy who couldn't let an old love go. And he was singing it in the car with Leah.

"We haven't done this in a long time," she said.

Her expression was vulnerable, her words on the border of…something. Surrender to questions about their past? All he knew was that it was the most vulnerable he'd ever seen her, which was saying a lot for someone behind the wheel of a car and an expression he couldn't fully see.

But even in a partial view, her smile did something to his insides. "It feels nice," he said.

"It does." She paused and he wondered what was going through her head. "I guess I'm glad your brother took your car?"

Right. Fortuitous circumstances brought on by…technical difficulties. "Me too," he said.

"So," she began as the music changed again. "What should I expect for tomorrow? Is it going to be like the expo where I show up with armor and a sword, ready to come to your aid?"

He laughed. "No," he said with a laugh. "I'm not...there yet. Heck, I don't know even if I'm there on the other side."

"Stop doubting yourself," she said. "You're amazing at what you do. You're picking up admirers—talented admirers—left and right. Carly's husband. Didn't he say that they got a mezuzah?"

He nodded. "Right." Bryce had repeated himself at the end of practice, and his wife, Carly—Leah's client—had said how much she loved the mezuzah.

Which was wonderful...such a great thing for him to hear. But this kind of professional validation wasn't what he was expecting for tomorrow.

He wasn't expecting hostility, per se, but... "This is different," he said.

"How? Same convention center, same exhibit space..."

"Different crowd," he replied. "It's entirely possible people will come up to the table and tell me that I have no place mixing streams like I do. That either I'm too much of a Jewish artist for lettering or too much of a secular person to be a sofer."

He couldn't see her face in the mirror, but he wondered what she was thinking. "So I'll need a sword and a history of comic books, then."

He blinked. "What?"

"I didn't forget everything I learned when we were together," she said with a laugh. "I know about how integral Jews were to the comics industry in the US and how many allegories for the Jewish diaspora are in famous stories told in the comics."

He nodded. "That's history and it's important, but there's been a problem in the last few years."

"What?"

She sounded genuinely concerned, as if he'd destroyed her idea of what comics were, and what the world he worked in was. "People are removing the Jewish heritage from those stories, and assuming Jews have no place in the industry."

"That's..." She shook her head. "It's awful."

"It is. Dejewification," he said as she pulled into the parking garage near his building, "and it doesn't have a solution, or it hasn't yet, because it keeps happening. I mean there are notable exceptions, Sam Moskowitz and Shadow Squad is one of them."

"This sounds sadly familiar," she replied.

"How so?"

"From what I know," Leah began after clearly thinking for a while, "Jewish athletes and artists are finding community as the industries they're a part of widen their reach and begin to search for voices from marginalized communities. Heck," she said with a laugh, "Melanie Gould herself can probably tell you what's going on in the romance genre with Jewish writers. Which isn't exactly the same as combatting what you're calling dejewification, but it's creating space in areas that hadn't actually acknowledged Jewish contributions previously."

He nodded. "I have heard of that," he said. "I guess people in comics have to reclaim that space, you know?"

Leah nodded. "You do," she said. "They're claiming space in hockey. If you see Asher you should probably ask him about that."

"Asher…?"

"Judith's fiancé."

He nodded. "Right." The other party of the ketubah he was making, the whole reason they'd been brought back into each other's orbits in the first place. "Thank you."

She smiled. "You're welcome."

It was nice collecting moments like these with Leah, sitting in her car, the windows down.

"So tomorrow? What time do you need to be there?"

And then they were back to business, back to planning. "Right. My signing's not till later, but I've found the doors are easier first thing."

Leah blinked. "When they open? I mean when the con opens for the day?"

He nodded. "Yeah. It's weird but that's when security's at its best." He did not mention the added benefit of being able to possibly spend the day with her.

"That's fine," she said, taking his argument about security without question; after all, she was ostensibly helping with crowd control, whatever exactly that was. "So tomorrow morning?"

He nodded. "It's Sunday so early will mean about ten, and my signing is about two? Three, toward the end."

"Can I kiss you before you go?"

"Kiss goodnight?" he said.

And she leaned over; he felt her lips on his, her hands, following the path of his stubble. And when she broke the kiss, the balm on his cheeks was cold. "So…"

"See you?"

"See you," he said as he left the car and headed upstairs, his head still spinning.

There was only one clear thought he could manage: Leah was amazing and if he didn't convince her he was worth taking another chance on, he didn't know what to do with himself.

Chapter Twelve

Event Three: Excelsior Comic Con, Manhattan Convention Center, New York

Purpose: Professional exposure for Samuel, exposure for the relationship, crowd control assistance from Leah

Leah wasn't surprised to see the complete change in the Expo Center from the last time she'd been there; heck, time-lapse footage showed baseball stadiums turning into outdoor hockey rinks, and indoor hockey rinks turning into basketball courts. All the convention center needed was a different set of lights, and the different posters supplied by the vendors and it was an entirely different place.

The mood was different too; people who walked the floor were wearing anything from extravagant costumes they must have spent tons of time on to random jerseys with the name of their favorite comic character on the back.

But the mood she was most focused on wasn't hers or the random passersby. It was Samuel's.

There was a bit of confidence in him when she saw him at the wedding expo, with his brother and the long line of people. It wasn't expected, but yet at the same time, he knew how to handle it.

This?

This was different.

He'd been quiet as they walked the floor, quiet as they found a space in the VIP area, quiet as they settled into breakfast and lunch and popped into panels.

"You want this?" she asked.

"I don't know what to do with myself," he replied, looking as if he'd forgotten how to behave in public. "I've never signed here."

She raised an eyebrow. "So you asked me here as a confidence booster, not crowd control?"

He didn't answer immediately, and she wondered what was going on in his head. "Not particularly. It's… I don't know what's going to happen."

"I can understand," she said. "Rookies have their first public appearances and they're not sure what to do. You can prepare for a moment all of your life, and then have it happen and, not be ready."

He laughed, but it wasn't bright. "I don't even know if this is the moment."

"You've been preparing for this since I've known you," she said before she realized what she was saying.

"Uhhh…"

Which was better than she expected him to say as they sat on folding chairs, eating con-floor hotdogs. Except for some reason, she decided she'd continue. Maybe it was because she wanted to see his confidence again. Maybe it was because she found a confident Samuel somehow more attractive…

No.

She was there for moral support, crowd control and to fulfill an obligation to her fake boyfriend. Not judge how attractive he may or may not be.

“You have been talking about comic con,” she continued, shoving words out of her mouth without really thinking about them, “being a part of it, here, since we were kids. You know what’s happening.”

“Signing here, yes,” he said. “I’m excited.”

“Then go with it,” she said. “Go with this. Be the guy you wanted to see when you were a kid, be as excited as you were about being here, waiting to see your favorites as you were back then.”

He nodded, and for once she was taken back to that place, back to that moment in elementary school where she’d seen his excitement up close and personal. The smile, the brightness of his eyes when he talked about letters and comics.

And this.

And as she stood in the corner, just outside the area where he was signing, she heard a voice.

“He’s going places.” Liam? Was that his name? Was that his mentor? “He’s going to get offers and he’s going to blow up. World’s ready for him, and I think he’s ready for the world."

She turned around to meet the man's eyes. "He's good," she said. "Really good."

"Glad he's got good support," Liam continued. "Family—his brother is great. And I consider myself a friend as well as a mentor. He's making great contacts, doing his thing."

Of course the surprise from Carly's brother-in-law Chris's excited reaction to seeing Samuel would never get old. Which made sense because Chris's wife was signing right next to Samuel.

"It's nice to see him realizing his own power," she replied, pulling the conversation back to where it needed to be. Because it was *nice* to see him realize his power, and Leah was comfortable enough saying that, whether he was her fake boyfriend or simply someone she used to know.

"It's nice to see that he's got you too," Liam replied. "Because the road he's on isn't going to be an easy one."

She didn't know how to respond to that. But later that night, when she'd gotten back to the safety of her apartment, she opened her bedroom closet, and pulled out a rather large package. It still sat in the wrapping paper she'd used so many years before, and she wondered if she'd ever give Samuel the graduation present she'd bought for him.

She also wondered whether even thinking about it was dangerous to her own psyche. Or her ability to stay emotionally uninvolved in the messy tangled threads that tied her and Samuel together.

Instead, she put the package down, closed the door and started to get ready for bed.

Chapter Thirteen

THE VERY LAST thing that Samuel expected on Monday morning was to be driving up to Rivertown with Liam and Oliver on the way to Bryce Emerson's house.

But Liam had called him early on Monday morning, explaining that Evan had called him, telling him that he had another friend who wanted to work with them.

"Who is it?" Samuel had asked, bleary-eyed, uncaffeinated and curious.

"Bryce Emerson? I've heard of him, but I don't…know him."

Threads, ties. He'd say this was fate, but he wouldn't call this anything like that. Just connections falling into place at the perfect time. Which meant he had to say something that felt strange. "Would it sound weird to say I do?" Samuel asked, slowly coming to life.

"It would be exciting," Liam replied, in a way that made Samuel feel the sentiment was genuine. Liam was like that. "Honestly, I don't have a clue and neither does Oliver, so it would be a very, very good thing professionally that one of us does, and personally as a mentor I love seeing you flourish."

After tamping down his enthusiasm at Liam's praise, Samuel was able to respond. "Good, hold that thought. Let me call you back."

Of course, Samuel was very lucky Bryce took his call; luckier still the conversation was quick. "Listen," he'd told Bryce, who wasn't exhausted, "we talked about doing something, and Evan Lefkowitz told my mentor…"

Bryce immediately said yes. "Evan called me yesterday, so I'm absolutely in to work with the logo team on a mask. Makes it look better for the organization but also for all of the artists, and reminding people why they're spending the money and who it's for."

Which was a relief that Evan had briefed someone in this group of potential collaborators. But instead of pondering this, he got directions and information from Bryce. Before calling Liam back.

"I'd offer to drive," Samuel said, "but my brother still has my car, and his car is in Briarwood."

"I'll take care of that," Liam said.

Not very long after, Samuel found himself in Oliver's car, heading up to Rivertown. Some of the houses reminded Samuel of parts of Briarwood, just yanked and dragged south down route nine, past Hollowville into a town with a river view.

"So how exactly did you meet this guy?" Liam asked. "Who is he?"

"He does multimedia," Oliver said, stepping in. "He

knows Isaac...most of his stuff is painting and sculpture, but I think he grabbed Evan's attention because of the hockey masks he makes."

Which was probably a more succinct explanation than Samuel could have made. "That's what he was talking about," Samuel said. "Some kind of mask. Anyway, he was at the Unicorns practice on Saturday. I guess his wife is one of the founders?"

"Oh that's great," Liam said, sounding impressed. "That's right, you told me you were going. So it was good in a bunch of ways then. Did you get some ideas?"

Samuel nodded. "I did," he said. "I'm excited to get to work on some of the concepts I have."

"Where was this practice?" Oliver asked. "How did you get in?"

"JCC in Briarwood. My girlfriend—" because that's what she was for all intents and purposes "—her niece was participating in a tryout session."

"Oh that's right. The practice was Leah's doing?" Liam said.

Samuel nodded, wondering what had happened on Sunday at the con, wondering what they'd said to each other. They seemed to have gotten along, but he wasn't sure.

"It was," Samuel finally said. "She had more than professional knowledge of the program."

"You still didn't say what the program was like," Liam said. "Tell us."

Samuel explained what he'd seen, the excited girls and the way the program incorporated very specific tools to make the fundamentals of the sport interesting to little girls with particular interests without compromising either the interests or the sport itself.

Seeing the excitement and the ideas fly across Liam's face made Samuel smile, not to mention the lack of judgment.

"We definitely should incorporate some of the kids and the moves into the logo," Oliver said.

Which was something Samuel himself had been playing with, so it felt good to have Oliver on board. "That's what I was thinking, at least," he admitted as they continued to drive through Rivertown, past the high school and signs that pointed to the downtown area. "But before we dive deeper, is there anything in particular that Evan Lefkowitz wants with the logo? Anything he doesn't want?"

Liam shook his head. "No," he said as they pulled into a long driveway. "Nothing in particular. Although we do have to decide whether it's going to be a logo general to the organization or specific to the gala. If we incorporate too many of the elements tied to the honoree, it won't be so much of a perpetual logo but something specific."

The conversation continued as they parked in the driveway and headed up to the front door. "Let's table this," Liam suggested.

Samuel nodded. "Bryce is going to want in to the discussion. He seemed excited to chat with us."

"That's good to know," Liam said as they headed up to the front door. They didn't even start to knock when Bryce opened the door.

"Welcome," Bryce said, his eyes sparkling. "Welcome to my humble abode."

"Thank you for hosting us," Samuel said, trying to take in the moment and enjoy himself. "I'm excited."

"It's no problem," Bryce replied, his smile wide. "You came out here to see me. So it's me who should be thankful."

"You have to be good to make us drive out to Yennevelt," Oliver said with a laugh. "Back of beyond..."

Samuel raised an eyebrow, slowly getting more comfortable. "You're from Crystal Harbor," he said. "Rivertown isn't Yennevelt and Briarwood is three towns over."

Liam clapped Oliver on the shoulder, a sign that Samuel had managed a successful jab. "My point exactly, though I wasn't the one who made it in the first place."

Thankfully, Bryce laughed and didn't shove the three of them outside. "Well I'm glad you're all here," he said. "Come on in. Let's go upstairs and figure this out."

"Upstairs?" Oliver asked.

Bryce nodded. "My wife's hockey space is downstairs. Better to block out the puck noises with the setup we've got. Safer too, that way. Also, there's better light in the attic."

"Great poetry," Samuel as he followed the group upstairs, trying not to trip on the stairs or someone's feet or anything like that. "Better living space?"

"The best."

And of course it was: light through the windows, drafting tables and equipment that went beyond the capacity of anything Samuel had ever imagined before. It was...beautiful.

Eventually, they settled down around a table at the center of the workspace. "So," Bryce asked. "What's the plan?"

"Well," Samuel said with a smile. "That's what we were hoping you'd help us figure out."

And as they dove in to the conversation they needed to have about what the logo would look like, he felt invigorated. Excited. He couldn't wait to start lettering.

LEAH GOT THE most random email that morning from one of her clients, asking her for a private meeting.

That was usual, but the name sending the email wasn't.

She'd just seen Carly on Saturday and she'd said practically nothing about meetings.

But Carly was a client who'd done her a major favor, and so she made the drive. The traffic was nonexistent by the time she got on the road, proving the theory that reverse commuting was still a thing.

What could be going on? What was happening?

She didn't know, and Leah pulled into the driveway, avoiding another car with New York plates that was parked off to the side. She didn't think much of it until she headed inside the house. "Thank you for coming," Carly said. "I'm very grateful that you drove all this way."

"You called me here," she said, as they headed to a small comfortable couch in the middle of the living room. "And it sounded urgent."

Carly nodded. "It is, Leah. Thank you for coming out here on such short notice."

"Not that short," Leah replied.

"Still," Carly said, "the fact that you're so willing to accommodate me is very much appreciated."

"It's what we do," Leah said with a smile as she took out her tablet. "So what's going on?"

"Well," Carly said, smiling, her eyes bright. "I'm ready to go back to training. I've talked to my doctor and I'm starting to stretch. Carefully. But stretching."

Carly was a goaltender, and she absolutely needed a doctor's approval or even supervision, before beginning to follow the specific pattern of stretching goaltenders required.

"That's wonderful," Leah said.

"It is. I'm excited to dive in. I'm being careful but I'm loving going back so far."

But within the words there were still questions. Carly was going back, but where? What was Carly's end goal? Instead of sitting and wondering, letting the words hang over them like clouds, Leah pushed forward. "Where do you want to end up?"

Leah held her breath as she waited for Carly's response; this was the key that would determine everything related to Carly going forward.

"The goal, I think," Carly finally said, "has always been to try to play with the Empires before my brother-in-law retires. I've always said that if I was going to do it, now was going to be the time."

This is why Carly wanted to have this conversation now. Because people were going to be asking questions about what Carly wanted at the gala.

Which meant her client had wanted to tell her first. "So," Leah said, trying to remember what the provision in the contract she'd signed look like. "You want to have the secret part of contract activate, and train with the Empires staff? See where you land? Make the decisions with them and then make moves?"

Carly nodded, relieved, as if she'd expected Leah to say something different. "That's what I want. And that's why you're here."

Leah could see the questions looming large in Carly's eyes. But it wasn't up to Leah to ask them; it was for Carly. "What do you want to know?"

"Do you think I have a chance?"

Which was the question that everybody wanted the answer to, including Leah herself. But knowing Carly, Leah elected to be as honest as she could. What were the facts she knew in the situation? She'd start there and go forward. "I think you and the Empires staff have always been clear that you playing with them, with the big club, has been the end goal of your arrangement with them. I think if you're ready to push back to high gear, this is the time to do it."

"Then it's perfect," she said.

"It is," Leah replied. And just as they started to talk more about specifics there was a loud whopping sound from upstairs. "What…?"

Carly laughed. "My husband has some artists over. Thankfully—" she pointed to a bassinette where a baby was sleeping peacefully "—Dana sleeps like the dead after a feeding so she's fine."

It was good to know the baby was sleeping, but Leah's mind had gotten stuck on a word. "Artists?"

Carly nodded. "Yeah. He's got a colorist, a letterer, and a guy who draws to collaborate on something."

Collaboration sounded great, but again, the skipping-record sound had played already. Because there weren't many people who lettered; it was very specialized job on the comics side. She had a feeling though, a thought made of a messy, knotted thread and a remembered bit of a conversation on Saturday.

She had a very strong feeling Samuel was part of the group that was collaborating upstairs.

But she had to ask. "Letterer?"

"Yeah," Carly said. "I think you know him actually… Was the guy you brought to practice on Saturday named

Samuel?"

"Yeah," she said. Because that's how life and messy tangled threads worked. At least for her. "It was."

"Oh great," Carly said. "They're doing some very cool stuff up there for the gala, actually."

And as she and Carly continued to talk, Leah wondered what was going on, and whether she'd want to stay long enough to see him.

A FEW HOURS later, Oliver and Liam had to go back to the city; but Samuel stayed behind to talk to Bryce about a few things. There was rideshare in Rivertown, after all, and he'd gotten a text from his brother about picking up his car at the shop over in Briarwood.

Eventually, they went down only to see Bryce's wife taking coffee cups into the kitchen. There was something off, and he could feel it in the way Bryce looked around, as if he wasn't seeing what he thought he would.

"I thought your agent was here," Bryce said.

Agent.

Carly's agent was…

Leah?

Yes. That's partially how Samuel got into the practice, and…

But he needed to say something. "Is she still…"

"Yeah," Carly said with a smile. "She went to the bathroom. We've taken the time to talk about a few things."

"Hi…"

And then anything Bryce or Carly said didn't matter. She was there and she was staring at him. Not a bad stare, no, but it was an inquisitive stare. What was he doing there? What was she going to ask him? What…

"I saw the others leave," she said. "You were still here, so you know."

Carly laughed, but he didn't care. Leah Nachman had *waited* for him. When she didn't have to. "Yeah," he said. "Finishing up a few things, having a quick chat."

"You heading back to the city?"

He wanted to say yes, but he couldn't. But then again he could give her something.

"Actually," he said with a smile. "Can you bring me somewhere in Briarwood?"

There was a long pause, and he wondered if he'd said the right thing or made the right choice. But she smiled. "Why not."

And as they said their goodbyes, he wondered how he'd managed this. Was it luck, friendship or something else?

Strings, threads, ties, things that tied them together. He'd follow them all the way to where they were going.

Chapter Fourteen

LEAH FOUND HERSELF in Briarwood for the second time that week; first, she'd dropped a grateful Samuel off at the mechanic's to pick up his brother's car, and now, she was at Shayna and Nathan's to drop off some of the hockey equipment that she'd found for Ramona.

"I'm in a pickle," she said, deciding to tell Shayna instead of her cousin or her sister. "I need a dress for the Tzedakah Exchange gala."

"Luckily for you," Shayna said as she grabbed her phone and purse, "I know a few people who know about dresses."

Leah, of course, was *not* surprised that after a few calls, Naomi and Judith both showed up, making excuses for Livvy as they sat in the car while Shayna drove across the county to the formal-wear shop she knew.

"This place is legendary," Naomi said with a grin. "How did you know this place?"

Leah had stopped being surprised by Shayna's random bits of arcane information a long time ago. But all the same, Shayna told the story about a dress of hers that had gotten stuck in customs. "They drove to new Jersey to get that dress," Shayna said with a smile. "And Leah needs a dress to impress. They also have a kids section, so I'll be getting Ramona something."

"Ramona's going?" Judith asked.

Shayna nodded and pulled into the parking lot. A furniture store, a huge bookstore and a few random shops flanked the store. "Yep. Her hockey team is making a presentation, or at least they'll be there to look adorable. So she needs a dress."

"Already?" Leah asked, then remembered the organizational philosophy. "I guess once a unicorn always a unicorn."

Shayna nodded. "Pretty much."

"Wait," Judith said, "is this the Tzedakah Exchange gala that you're going to?"

Leah nodded. "Yeah." The Jewish charity organizations were way too close for comfort in most cases, and the last thing she wanted to know was that her sister was going. But she asked anyway, maybe just to be polite. "You going?"

"Yeah," Judith said, much to Leah's chagrin. "Asher's officially going, and I'm his plus-one."

Which made sense; her client and future brother-in-law had begun an organization that worked with Jewish hockey players five years before.

Yet another hurdle she'd deal with at the gala, and heading toward it.

Great.

SAMUEL HATED THE rules for suits, but there were benefits to having a brother-in-law who paid attention to fashion.

Tommy directed him first to his favorite store, and once he'd bought the suit, his brother-in-law led the reluctant trio out of the city and to a tailor who would make sure that whatever garment he brought in would be altered in time for the gala.

"Why are we going to Westchester?" Aaron asked as they pulled into the shopping center parking lot, which was the question that Samuel wanted to ask, except Samuel wasn't interested in incurring the wrath of someone who was helping him.

"The guy's practically retired," Tommy said. "But he's here, with a few of his relatives, and enjoying himself."

"Don't question it," Samuel said. "He got me a suit."

"That I did," Tommy said as they headed toward the store, unassuming as it was.

"Hi," Tommy said as they opened the door. "Tommy Levine-Goldfarb. Mottel's expecting me."

The woman who met them nodded, and shortly, an older man emerged from the back.

"Hello, Mottel," Tommy said, gesturing. Which Samuel figured was his cue. He figured correctly, thankfully, because the next move was to point. "My brother-in-law needs to be fitted for an event."

The older man didn't say anything, just waved his arms and pointed toward the dressing rooms.

And so, deciding that this was even more of his cue, Samuel followed, going into the fitting room and putting the suit on.

"Guy's brilliant," Tommy said.

As he came out of the dressing room, the older man looked him up and down. "A few small adjustments," Mottel said as he came out of the dressing room. "You will be good." And as Mottel began pinning and pulling, out of the corner of his eye, Samuel saw a vision.

A short jacket over a dress, fitting curves that went on for days, blue eyes that met his, chestnut hair with a hint of a curl.

Leah.

He gulped.

Leah Nachman had always been pretty; then and now. But right now, at this moment…she…

"Abba," a voice said, breaking through his concentration, "you took my tape measure and the last time you did that I told you I'd have to do my next fitting where your extra tape measure is. So *hineni*."

And hineni meant that whoever this was, was going to have Leah stand up on a stool right across from him to do her fitting.

"Hi," she whispered, her voice carrying across to where he stood. "Awkward though."

He tried not to full-on laugh; he managed just to snort. "Could be worse," he said.

"I don't know how."

And then as he watched the woman start to pin and pull and push and sigh, he decided he didn't want to know.

"Like this?"

He laughed. There was something about having dual fittings, standing side by side, co-conspirators in weird embarrassment, that brought them closer. "Don't want to think about it," he finally said.

"Why are you here?"

"My brother-in-law," he said, resisting the urge to run his hands through his hair. "He knows clothing and he knows this place. You?"

"My sister-in-law," she replied. "I realized I didn't have the right outfit for the gala. My niece is up in the kids section getting fitted with my sister and my sister-in-law. And Naomi."

"Your niece is going? To the gala?"

Leah nodded. "She's a member of the team being honored, even though it was her first session, they take them in immediately. So she's going."

In the space between what she said and what he wanted to say, he heard a screech and then some familiar voices that made him cringe.

"What's going on?" she whispered.

He shrugged, then heard a commotion of voices. Including one very familiar one.

Aaron.

AS IF STANDING and getting fitted across from Samuel wasn't enough, hearing her cousin Naomi's screech amidst the commotion put the cherry on her shit sundae. "Hi, Naomi," she managed.

As if it couldn't get worse, Naomi didn't turn toward her but toward someone else. "Aaron Levine-Goldfarb, how are you?"

"I," Samuel's brother said, "am good. What brings you here?"

Leah tried not to scream as Chava, the tailor, stabbed her with a pin.

"Stop moving! If you stopped moving, then I wouldn't stab you."

"Sorry," she managed. But her cousin's arrival couldn't be at a worse time, and she needed to say something about it. "Naomi…what the heck?"

Naomi seemed smug. "Ramona's adorable but there are only a few people who can watch a four-year-old pick a dress before things get chaotic. And then I remembered you were here. So here I am."

And without warning, her cousin came closer. Leah felt like she'd been placed under a microscope, as Naomi inspected every inch of her body. "You need a magnifying glass?"

Naomi shook her head, in no way chagrined. "I like the dress," her cousin finally pronounced. "And your boyfriend there?"

Of course Naomi was going to say something.

"Boyfriend?"

A guy she didn't know but figured was Aaron's husband, the source of the Goldfarb in the last name.

"Still?" Naomi asked.

"Yeah," she managed. "Still."

"Interesting." Naomi looked across the room. "You guys going to the gala together?"

"You should go together," Aaron of course. "It would be a great idea."

"Two nice people," Mottel said. "Going to the same event, who are going to look nice? Why should you not go together?"

Samuel looked back at her; they hadn't actually finalized their plans. "So I guess we're going?"

"Yeah, your plus-one or mine?" Leah said, relaxed in a situation where she shouldn't be, considering the questions that would come her way between then and when the gala would actually take place.

Then again, if she couldn't survive this situation with Samuel, what was she doing fake dating him in the first place?

Chapter Fifteen

"I GOT ROPED into helping organize," Liam had said when Samuel answered the call the morning of the gala. "Speaking of which, we may need some hands. You up for it?"

Of course, the only answer for that was 'yes.'

He'd been to the hotel and the ballroom before; it was a great location—high ceilings, sculpted walls—but now it was chaos. Tables and signs and people dropping things off, all signs of an impending event. And for the next few hours, Samuel found himself in the midst of that chaos, lifting and carrying all sorts of items from the arrival table to the requested locations until he needed a breather and a bottle of water.

As he took a swallow, he found himself with the odd realization that loading art for an auction taking place in the middle of a gala was oddly similar to loading in at an expo. Especially if the gala was a charity gala and the proceeds from it went to the charity organization being honored.

"We need some help over there," Liam said. "Break time is over."

Following where Liam was pointing, Samuel could see three guys were doing their best to maneuver a sculpture past an entrance. It was on a dolly cart and very, very, very unstable.

"They don't just need help," he managed. "They need a miracle."

"And we—" Liam grinned as they headed across the room "—are their miracle."

When they got there, one of the guys pushing the sculpture straightened up, stepped away from the dolly cart.

"Thank you, Liam, for saving the day," said *the one and only* Isaac Lieberman in a tone that reminded Samuel exactly where he was and what he was doing. Hero worship went out the window, replaced with the understanding that he was *help* at that moment, as opposed to a random person.

"Well, totally not a problem," Liam said, pointing a thumb in his direction. "My assistant and I are here to save the day."

"And you are?"

"Samuel Levine," he said.

"Oh right," Isaac replied with a smile. "You made my ketubah, and the mezuzah."

His brain stopped completely as he digested the information Isaac was giving him. "Uh…"

Liam said, "You are not only talented, but unaware of how talented you are. You're also being mentored by me so I'm taking you to great places."

"He knows what he's doing," Isaac said, approval in his tone, even as Samuel tried to keep himself tethered to the earth.

"These two," Isaac continued, "are driving me nuts."

"Over there?" Liam asked, in the tone of someone who was trying to get a hold of the situation.

Isaac nodded, and Samuel followed Isaac's gesture only to see the two guys standing around the sculpture. One dark-haired guy and one lighter-haired one. "Abe," he said pointing to the lighter-haired guy, "lift there maybe."

"Got it," the man said.

"That spot," Isaac continued, having taken control so even Liam stepped back. "I think that's sensitive, so Jacob you move over there."

This time, the dark-haired guy nodded. "Steady hands win the race, huh?"

As they watched the two guys get into position, there was a moment where they were getting their hands into place.

"Don't drop it," Isaac said, shaking his head before he turned toward Liam. "Can you cover the back end?"

It took a bit to get them all situated; Isaac and his two friends, and Liam and Samuel, but they were just about ready to lift when another voice split the silence.

"I cannot believe," said the voice he recognized but couldn't quite place, "that one sculpture has this motley crew lifting it."

"Are you going to jaw at us, Evan?" one of the guys (Jacob, was it?) said. "Or are you going to help lift this?"

Evan. Evan Lefkowitz?

Right. The guy he met at Leah's cocktail party, who most likely would get a kick out of all of this.

But he couldn't let his mind whirl at the possibilities because the sculpture needed to be lifted.

"On three," Isaac said.

And when Isaac reached the count of three, Samuel lifted his part of the sculpture, holding his breath, doing his best to play his role in the movement.

Finally, they settled the sculpture and took a breath.

"Now I can say a proper hello. How are you, Samuel? I love the logo, by the way."

"I'm glad to hear," he said, feeling pride run around his chest. "I really enjoyed the process."

"I also like the synergy with Bryce's mask," Evan said, "and if you haven't seen it, make a point of stopping over there tonight."

Samuel nodded. "I will."

"Good," Evan said. "It's rare I get to do an event like this," Evan continued. "Tzedakah Exchange does a lot of different things but usually with adults, usually focused on the arts as opposed to sports. Anyway, we need to talk more if that's something if you're interested in."

He nodded. "I'd love to."

"Okay," Liam said, "my *mentee* and I have to get changed and settled. Then we'll come down and enjoy the gala."

"And wow," Evan said with a laugh, "now I know I've been dismissed by my old soccer buddy. You better come down, Hernandez. I know where to find you."

Liam smirked, and as Samuel followed him out of the room, he hoped he'd be able to manage the obligations of the evening without losing his mental facilities.

THERE WERE MANY different reasons Leah was very glad she hadn't spent the money to hire a hairdresser or a makeup artist for the night. One of which was that she needed her cousins with her for support as she put on her armor.

She'd picked up the dress from the dress shop recommended by Shayna and it fit her like a glove. "Gorgeous," Naomi said before wrapping a towel around her shoulders. "Now let me work my magic."

As Naomi did her thing, finishing off the makeup, Leah thought about what the evening would be like: business, social, family and Samuel. She was now in a situation that mixed them more and more, tangling them in a web she hoped she'd be able to separate at some point.

Soon.

"You look gorgeous," Naomi said with a flourish as she put the makeup brush down.

Leah knew how to put on makeup, but Naomi was more of a professional. "Thanks," she said.

And as she headed toward the mirror, Leah took a long look at herself. Naomi's artistry on her face was just…flawless. The dress was a pale pink and went down to her ankles, hugged her curves. Her hair was glossy, dark and gorgeous, courtesy of Liv, who was a queen with a straightener. "I love you guys," she gushed.

"We love you more," Naomi said. "You are going to shine. Who's coming to get you?"

"Shayna and Ramona because Samuel is busy doing stuff."

Which was when she heard the knock at the door.

"Go get him," Naomi said.

"You've got your armor on," Liv said. "He will not be able to withstand the gorgeousness. All you have to do is be vulnerable for a little. Let him see you."

"This isn't just date night," she said, trying not to snort. "This is also work for me. My client is being honored," she said as she gathered up her stuff. Put her wrap across her shoulders and grabbed her bag.

There was another knock at the door, and this time she could hear the giggles.

"I think," she said with a laugh, "my ride is getting impatient."

Liv opened the door, only to see Shayna and Ramona waiting. "Are you ready, Auntie Leah?" Ramona asked.

"I am," she said. "Are *you* ready for tonight?"

And as they headed into the car and Shayna buckled

Ramona into her car seat, Ramona talked about her dress and how her hockey team was going to help present the award to 'Miss Carly.'

"Do you have a plan, Leah?" Shayna asked. "Or are you just going to wing it?"

"Plan? For?"

"Samuel."

"Samuel's not the only reason I'm going," she said, reminding Shayna and herself. "Carly's my client."

"Which is true. Carly's being honored."

"By all Unicorns! The whole team. All of them," Ramona said from the back of the car.

"Woow," Leah said with a smile, exaggerating the word on purpose. "That's wonderful. I'm excited for her and all of you. Do you have a speech to give?"

"No speech," Ramona said. "I'm four."

"No." Shayna laughed. "You missed the event five years ago when your big brother Shim spoke at Asher's opening banquet."

"But unlike with Asher and my sister," Leah replied, "it's going to be interesting to see how I manage a date night with Samuel, who's also got professional obligations, as well as act as a professional agent representing the firm along with Carly."

"You're going to do great," Shayna said. "Ramona and I are here to support you, and you know that Judith and Asher will run any sort of interference, and anything else you might need."

As they pulled up to the entrance, Leah wondered exactly how this was going to go, and hoped for the best.

And not a tangled web.

Chapter Sixteen

SAMUEL WONDERED WHO made the rules about ties. He absolutely hated them, everything about them, but for some reason, he wasn't the sort of person who could pull off a suit or blazer or whatever without one. Which was fine.

Sort of. As long as he didn't pull it so tight that he'd choke. But the suit was fantastic. Mottel the tailor was as good, if not better than promised.

"I like this location," Liam said.

And it was ready for a party. The chaos they'd seen before while the two of them had been organizing in different capacities had fallen away to reveal the best of what an event space could be. The high ceilings, Grecian columns, and the gorgeous floors were decked out in the colors of the organization, even before they stepped inside the ballroom where the gala was being held.

Just outside the ballroom itself, their logo appeared in large banners, the largest he'd ever seen his work displayed.

"It is nice," he said.

"You better get used to this kind of praise," Liam said laughing. "You're impressing everybody, including some execs. Pencil some space for me in the next few days, hm?"

He was already over the place but at the same time, he could barely decipher what Liam said. "What?"

"You're catching everybody's attention," Liam said. "Everybody in the art and print world at least. Apparently you're *the* ketubah writer for comic art people."

"Which is news to me," he managed, knowing that a conversation thanking his brother for separating him from knowledge of his ketubah and mezuzah clients specifically would absolutely need to be forthcoming. But Liam didn't need to know that. "I think you could have knocked me over with a feather when Isaac told me."

"And you impressed Evan Lefkowitz, and Bryce Emerson is collaborating with you. All you needed was confidence," Liam said. "And maybe a direction."

"And a good mentor," he said to Liam.

"Who," Liam replied, "now believes you're ready for the next phase of your career, and you need to pencil some time for me in your schedule either the end of this week or anytime next, for me to guide you into it."

There were very few words he could think of, things he wanted to say but didn't have the words for, standing in his suit and tie. But thank you worked no matter what. "Thank you," he managed.

Liam nodded. "You're welcome," he said. "Now let's go."

And as they headed inside, he wasn't sure whether it was

anticipation or dread that filled him more.

THE VALET PARKING was the perfect option for Shayna's purposes. "Last thing I want to worry about tonight, with," her sister-in-law said as she pointed to the excited little girl who wanted to get out of her car seat, "is where I put my car."

Which made a lot of sense. "And the parking ticket?"

"Goes right into the bag with everything else I don't have to worry about until it's necessary."

Which also made a lot of sense. But more importantly, her sister-in-law looked fantastic, as did little Ramona, who'd probably incorporated more than a little bit of glitter into her nail polish, and her dress.

Yep, she thought as she grinned at her niece. Adorable.

This was going to be a good night.

But when she looked up, she could see the Tzedakah Exchange banners and the logos hanging from the top of the building.

"Unicorn!" Ramona said as she pointed up at the banners.

And yes. The banners had unicorn hoofprints, and the letters themselves, if you looked close enough, were microcalligraphy, except the foundations of the letters were...unicorn horns.

This was what Samuel had been working on at Carly's with Bryce, what he'd come up with after going to practice.

Genius.

"You there?"

Leah nodded. "Yeah. Just admiring the art." And thinking about the artist, but she wasn't telling her sister-in-law that.

"Tell him," Shayna said before she turned sharply toward Ramona who had started to make her way toward one of the larger banners. "You will hold my hand or we will go home. You will stay with me. Is that understood?"

Ramona, suitably chastened, nodded her head. "Yes, Ima. I'll stay."

"Good." Shayna grinned. "Now that's settled, where were we? Ah yes. You will tell that man how you feel. And enjoy this night; this isn't just work, even though I know it is for you."

Which was the best advice she could consider.

"You ready to go in, take this place by storm?"

She laughed. "I don't know about storm, but I'm as ready as I'm going to be."

"Good," Shayna said as she took out her phone. "I need to get Ramona to an entrance in about ten minutes, so I have to head in. Are you going to be okay?"

Leah nodded. "I've got business too, so I'll see who's here? Check the lay of the land? Schmooze for the agency, keep the balls in the air and all of that good stuff?"

"Sounds good," Shayna replied. "Keep in touch if there's something happening that I need to know."

"Will do," she said. And as Shayna headed into the gala to try and bring Ramona to where her hockey team was gathering, Leah found her way into the room. She could mingle with the best of them; it was her job, of course. Part of it at least. She also had been to enough events in these overlapping circles of Jewish charities and organizations to know at least some of the players.

As she walked through the room she thought about the possibility of asking the Empires for a crisis PR rep on call, so that they could handle whatever issues came up with social media and any other sports angle when Carly made the move.

Which was something else she could think about as she searched for Samuel. Just as she arrived at the auction space, she saw a very familiar pair of cocoa brown eyes, a soft yet firm jawline, and dark hair that had the beginnings of gray.

The scariest part was that she didn't have to remind herself she liked the way Samuel looked in the suit he'd been fitted for alongside her that night in Westchester. She just *did.* A sudden heat rose up from her toes and through her veins as if it was a reflex.

Samuel Levine was gorgeous.

And she was in even deeper trouble.

LIAM HAD SEEN someone he needed to talk to, and so he'd gone off, leaving Samuel by himself.

Which was okay as this was how it was supposed to go; he wasn't supposed to be the baby chick idling behind his mentor's wing. He looked at the map of the room they'd printed before heading toward the area that had been reserved for the auction items.

A set of tables in rows of two were lined up across the back corner of the room. As he headed toward them, he could see the large Isaac Lieberman sculpture that he'd helped to move in.

He stopped, gazing in awe at the mask Bryce Emerson had made using the ideas and inspiration they'd all shared. And felt so proud, so excited. But as he turned to walk down the aisle containing some of the signed books and experience items, he looked up into a very familiar pair of blue eyes.

Leah.

His reaction was instantaneous and unstoppable, as if his entire body took notice of the way the dress she wore fitted her curves perfectly. He couldn't help but stare.

Her hair was long and glossy, and her eyes sparkled.

"Hi," she said.

It took him a second for him to register she'd spoken, as if once again he'd gotten lost in the lines of her body. "Hello," he finally replied.

She bit her lip; Leah Nachman never bit her lip in front of him, not when they were young, and not any time since.

She was *never* nervous in front of him and he wondered if this was the moment they were letting their guards down.

His first impulse was to blow out a breath, but he held it in and spoke his mind. "You're gorgeous," he said.

"Strategic tailoring," she replied with a laugh.

He remembered how that tailoring had happened; how they'd shared a moment in that shop in Westchester. "No," he said.

She glanced at him for a moment and that look hit him deep. Blue eyes bearing down, seeing right through him. "You find what you're looking for?"

This was where it got confusing, this dance they were doing. "I'd say I did," he replied, "but then you'd look for the wrappers or the string."

She raised an eyebrow. "I have no idea what you're saying."

Not a bad thing, just confusion, thankfully. "Cheese," he replied. "Maybe I'm layering on the cheese a little too thick."

She shrugged, the lines of her shoulders fluid and soft. "Maybe, but not tonight." She paused and he wondered where she was going, what she was thinking.

What she thought of him.

No.

Not that far, not yet at least.

"You came with your mentor?"

He nodded. "Yeah. He headed off, something about people in the crowd. You?"

"My sister-in-law," she said with a laugh. "There's nothing like coming to a late-night event during the summer with an excited four-year-old."

"Sugar?"

"A lot of it," she replied. And then she paused. "I saw the signs. The logo, the lettering is gorgeous."

"Thanks," he said, trying to keep himself together at the praise. "I had fun watching them practice, so I tried to put their energy into the logo. Do you want to see something?"

She raised an eyebrow, and he wondered if she thought he was deflecting. "Sure..."

He nodded, took the hand she reached out, hoping he wasn't sweating through his palms, and walked her back down the display area to the mask Bryce had made.

He loved looking at it, loved seeing the microcalligraphy and the paint.

"This is beautiful," she managed. "This is what he was working on?"

He nodded. "Yep. That's what he was working on the day you did me the favor of driving me to the mechanic."

She laughed quickly but composed herself. "I see the touches in the lettering," she said, her fingers resting inches from the glass display case. "I can see the synergy with the logo. Deliberate?"

He nodded. "Yeah. Very much so."

"So," she asked, making him slightly nervous. "Did you find your place card?"

He shook his head. "No. I haven't." Which was probably the safest statement he could make, but he wasn't sure.

She nodded. "Let's go figure this out," she said.

And what made him more excited, was that she didn't let his hand go. Just continued to hold on to it as they left the auction space, fingers entwined.

Bashert.

OF COURSE, IT turned out that Leah was sitting at a table with Samuel; she wasn't going to complain—they were supposed to be sitting together for many reasons, but primarily because they were 'dating.'

Rumors traveled fast, and people knew too many people for her to believe otherwise. And the conversation that naturally sprung up about industries and strange collaborations they both remembered was fun. One in particular that tied hockey and comics together ignited memories that were inspirations in the good times, like the way she was letting this one be.

"Do you remember that collaboration?" he asked her, his fingers clearly tight against his fork, his knuckles the pale white of toothpaste.

So she nodded, brushing a finger against his, allowing herself to remember what they'd been when the collaboration took place—dating. Because it had happened back when they were in high school. "I do," she said, remembering the package in the closet.

He smiled, and she'd never been immune to Samuel's smile. "I was excited about it."

She remembered.

"I remember how you told me how historic this collaboration was," she said.

Luckily his comment wasn't picked up by the rest of the group, because the last thing she wanted was to follow him down memory lane and rehash her private memories…in public.

But as the music changed, some of the group, headed toward the dance floor. She debated going to the bar for a drink; instead she stayed in her seat. So did Samuel.

Right next to her.

He wasn't close enough for his pants to touch her dress, but she was thinking of it, moving just slightly to…

Something pulled her out of whatever trance was going on in her head, and when she met Samuel's beautiful brown eyes, she saw a question there.

Yet she didn't know this version of him well enough to figure out what he wanted. So she just sat there, looking at him.

"Do you want to go?"

Go.

What? Leave…

No. It was too early and he couldn't be asking that, especially before the auction.

Which meant the realization of what he was actually asking her hit her hard. Dance. She was being asked to join the group who'd gone to the dance floor. "Do you dance?"

He laughed, and she tried not to laugh along with him. His laughs had always been contagious and clearly that hadn't changed either.

"Not well," he said, answering her question and letting his drop. "But well enough to dance to a string quartet."

A string quartet that had just finished playing a song about lost love, and the hope that when a relationship ended, one partner would remember the other in their best moments. That wasn't a song she wanted to dance to. She didn't want to glorify hope of being remembered.

But the music changed again, the first notes of a song she loved, about strength. About how love couldn't hurt the singer anymore because they'd encased themselves in a metal shield. She'd stopped being surprised about the ability of string quartets to turn the most powerful songs into softer ones, all the while keeping their essence.

"Let's," she said. "Let's go."

He offered his hand then. She took it without questioning, letting her fingers get as tangled up in his as she was getting in him, and let him take her to the floor.

There were people around but she didn't look to see who she knew; where her sister or sister-in-law or niece or future brother-in-law were. She just followed him. And when they arrived at a spot on the floor, he bowed.

She wasn't sure what to make of that; was it honesty or was it just following the protocols of the waltz they were about to mangle? She threw the concern out of her head as they slowly moved into the dance, sliding back and forth, his arms encasing her, his warmth filling her.

Leah held Samuel's hands, those long fingers, as they twirled with everybody else in the crowd, his motions matching hers, even as she moved back and forth to a dance that required clasped hands to one that encouraged her hips to shake.

She didn't care who watched her, didn't care who saw what was happening. She just…was.

And they melded, merged, his hand was there to dip her when it was time, his fingers grasping hers as he took her into a twirl. Being lost with him in the center of the floor and the music…

When she realized it was over, there was only one thing she could do.

She drew her fingers along his cheekbones, feeling the immense power of his stare upon her. "Do you…wish?"

"I do…I mean you may…" He shook his head and leaned toward her, pressed his lips to hers and simply blew her mind. His lips, the way his mouth fell against hers, was overpowering in the best of ways. The way his hands followed the path of her shoulders as if he hadn't forgotten her…

Then she remembered, as if cold water had burned the fire of memory. "We can't do this," she said.

"Tell me why," he said. "What's going on?"

"This is business…you have too many contacts," she managed, "I have too many contacts, too many people…I just can't."

He nodded. "I'm not going to push," he said, fully aware of the need to let a conversation thread drop. "But they all know we're dating at this point."

"Mauling you in public at a gala like this isn't right though."

"Right," he said.

She led him off the floor, doing her best to keep up appearances; she wore the professional mask, even though she once again held his hand, her fingers tangled in his. She looked like she'd been kissed; that was fine, but practically removing his clothes on the dance floor like she was going to would not have been fine in any way shape or form, no matter how many people knew they were together.

And yet at the very same time, she found herself upset that she couldn't kiss him more. Kissing him would be dangerous.

This time, she'd almost lost her mind.

Hopefully the change of scenery, the jolt in her brain, would be enough to keep her from forgetting why dating him for real was a horrible idea.

Chapter Seventeen

SLIGHTLY OUT OF it, still lost in the haze that always had been the aftermath of kissing Leah, Samuel let her lead him to the bar. "You need a drink?" he asked as he ordered himself the first thing that came to mind.

She nodded, ordering some blue drink that the bartender had made the central theme.

"This feels…right," he said.

"It feels like a mistake," she replied.

Leah wasn't someone who publicly made a deal about how she felt; she'd always lived behind walls and in order to be around her, she had to feel comfortable enough to let them down. That, or be comfortable with the consequences when she built them back up minutes if not mere seconds after she let them down.

And clearly it…the walls, the whatever…was his own fault. He'd been a ridiculous little shit, not used to actually dealing with his own problems in ways that were healthy.

"Sir?"

He shook his head, accepted the whiskey from the bartender and raised it toward where Leah stood.

"L'chaim," she said as she clinked her glass with his.

"L'chaim." To life. Traditional toast, a bond they shared. At least it was something.

"To taking chances," she said.

"Chances?"

"Dating. Faking, contracts. Those chances."

He nodded. Walls. Ever present.

"How about we head back to the table?" Leah said, holding out her hand.

He took it, and he could barely keep his head on straight as Leah wrapped her fingers around his. He hoped she was having as difficult a time as he was.

IT FELT LIKE her hand was burning as she took Samuel past the bar and away from the table, toward the balcony that was part of the gala set up.

The summer breeze was lovely, and honestly, more than a drink, she needed air. She needed to cool down, to calm down. Slow down the slamming of her heart and throw ice cubes on the fact she was sweating.

"This is nice," he said.

And it was. Somehow, the owners of the building had managed to recreate an oasis in the middle of the city, allowing the patrons of the establishment to feel as if they were separated from time and existence. That's what she needed to remember. "This is…safe," she said.

"I take it we're not?"

"You're…going to make this impossible."

"This?" he asked as if she'd stumped him. "What are you talking about and how am I making it impossible?"

"Fake dating. Our arrangement."

"But this isn't the first time in the midst of this…that we kissed. We fit," he said.

She nodded. "I know that," she replied, holding back the feelings that were threatening to explode. "We've managed to convince everybody we need to convince that we're dating, mostly…but we're getting into trouble."

He looked at her. "What…what do you mean by trouble?"

"What we did on the dance floor."

He didn't respond, and she tried not to notice the haze leaving his eyes. "I'm not sure where you're going with this."

"We were devouring each other in public in the middle of a…gala that you and I are attending for work reasons."

The words were stark and clear, her desperate attempt to draw a boundary, and her heart pounded through her chest as she waited for a reaction.

He nodded, making her feel as if he was tracing the lines of her face with his eyes. Touching her in ways she didn't want to consider. "Okay?"

"There are other ways of showing affection that don't involve kissing," she said making sure he was watching her as she took his hand, traced the lines of his palms with her fingers. "You don't have to swallow my tongue in public to show me I matter."

"Mmm," he said, the sound a strange cross between a growl and a purr, and he moved to wrap his fingers around hers. "I see."

"We're still a mess," she said, as she leaned into his touch. "We don't know how to talk."

"Mmm," he managed. "That's because what we need to talk about has been removed from consideration."

"Can versus need to," she said. "Should versus having no business to. Which is why we can't actually date."

"We still go up like fireworks when we get near each other," he said, notably still not letting up on her hand. Granted she didn't stop touching him either. "Much to the anger, surprise, and annoyance of both of us."

"Chemistry was never a problem," she said.

"No," he said. "It's still not."

She wasn't sure who leaned forward first, who closed the space between them, but before she knew it, her lips were touching his, her breath on his face, his breath intertwined with hers like a Havdalah candle.

As if that acknowledgment that their chemistry had nothing to do with their conversation freed her from implications.

"Leah!"

Shayna.

Shit.

"Leah," her sister-in-law said again. "Ramona had to go but she wanted to make sure you were watching her and I couldn't find you..."

"Well," Leah said with a snort as Samuel straightened himself up out of the corner of her eye. "You have found me."

"I also," Shayna continued, "thwarted Judith who wanted to come after you."

"And this," Leah said, "is why I love you."

Which was when she turned to Samuel. "Should we head back in?"

He nodded. "We should."

She stood, allowed him to take her hand, hoping she didn't look like she'd had a run-in with an air dryer. And then, her hand in Samuel's, Leah followed Shayna inside.

SAMUEL FOUND HIMSELF lost in thought as he and Leah were leaving the gala. The display had been gorgeous, the little unicorns were cute, even though they were clearly exhausted; Leah's niece had fallen asleep on her mother's shoulder as they were waiting for the car.

But what stayed stuck in his mind like a broken record was the speech.

There had been a very obvious reason why, aside from

embarrassment, that Leah's sister-in-law came to get Leah.

Carly, Leah's long-term client, had made sure to mention Leah's name in the speech she gave when accepting the award.

"I want to thank my agent, Leah Nachman," Carly had said, "for supporting me, and inspiring me. I don't think I'd ever be here without her. I don't think it would be possible to be standing here and thinking about my future the way I am if I didn't have someone like Leah in my corner."

And Samuel was so proud of Leah.

Could he say that?

Could he say that he was so proud of the career Leah had built? Could he say that he was so ridiculously proud of what she'd done with her life, and what she continued to do?

Could he tell her that she inspired him?

"I hear the gears turning," she said, turning in his direction. "Tell me."

He raised an eyebrow, wondering. What would she say?

"Come on," she said. "Spill it. I've known you too long to not realize that you have something to say. So I'll listen."

He'd known her long enough to know that she wasn't going to stop asking, knew she'd be relentless unless he said something she'd believe. So he nodded, looked into her gorgeous blue eyes and said it. "You inspire me."

She didn't say anything at first, but she didn't move either; he'd consider that a plus.

"You asked," he said.

"I know."

He laughed. "You regret asking?"

"Honestly?"

He nodded.

"No. You were staring at me," she said, running a free hand through her hair. I was worried it was something creepy."

He laughed. "I'm glad you didn't think what I said was creepy."

"No," she said. "I didn't. It felt good to hear that from someone who's where you are in your career."

Which felt strange and almost like a cop-out.

Except it was from Leah.

She wasn't copping out.

She was saying something on a different level than she had in a long time, saying something emotional, and using his career to do it.

So he didn't complain, didn't whine, didn't yell.

All he did as they headed out of the gala space, hand in hand, was say, "You're welcome."

Chapter Eighteen

SAMUEL'S VOICE RANG in Leah's head for the entire night after the gala. From him waiting with her until Ramona and Shayna headed off, from him walking her to the rideshare car she'd order, then getting in with her.

"You don't have to," she said, even though she didn't want to admit to herself that it felt nice to be like this with him.

"I…you know."

"You'll worry," she said, smiling, cupping his cheek with fingers she knew weren't sweating, even though her heart was pounding.

"I will," he said before correcting himself. "I would."

His chocolate brown eyes practically caressed her in ways that his fingers clearly weren't going to in the back of the car. His hands settled in hers as she put her head on his shoulder.

He was comfortable.

Waaaay too comfortable.

Which meant sending him back to his apartment when they pulled up by hers was the right decision, putting him back in the rideshare with a "Now I'll worry. Text me when you get there?"

"Absolutely," he said. "Soon as I step over the threshold."

Hours later, the look in his eyes haunted her and his voice played in her head like a song.

As did the text he'd sent her.

I'm okay. I had a great time tonight.

She tried to remind herself she wasn't actually dating him, that it was a situation where she only needed to see his text and not respond to it.

But her fingers didn't listen to anything, nor did her heart. All those parts of her paid attention to was the tangled web that was bringing her closer to Samuel, and the need to respond to his text.

Glad you got back okay. I'm tired, but I had a great time tonight too.

She wasn't staring at her phone, wasn't wondering whether he was responding.

Didn't hope he was going to respond.

Talk to you soon. Goodnight.

The next thing she knew, she woke up with the phone in her hand, that text from him in front of her. And the blaring alarm from her calendar entry that said she'd promised Liv, Judith and Naomi that she'd meet them in Briarwood.

But all she could see was the look in Samuel's eyes when he left in the rideshare.

"You're here," Naomi's voice broke through her daydreams. "Earth to Leah. Earth to Leah."

Leah blinked, looking around Briarwood's main street.

She and Naomi were heading toward Liv, who was supervising the opening of something Leah vaguely remembered was called Briarwood's 'Main Street Block Party.' "I'm here," Leah said. "Trust me I'm here."

"Which is fascinating," Naomi replied, "because up until a few minutes ago, I didn't think you were mentally here, just a shell of a body."

Weird, but so was the situation. "So what's exactly going on again? Because Judith has a meeting…?"

"Judith always has meetings these days." Naomi said, "Or do you not realize your sister is incapable of slowing down even though she wants you to settle down."

"It's saved me," she said with a smile. "I don't think we've been able to sit down and have conversation, a real one, since the expo."

"Saved you?" Naomi asked.

"So what's this whole thing actually?" Leah asked. "Because I clearly wasn't paying attention when Liv explained it."

Naomi snickered. "Riight. I'll give you this one because you admit to not paying attention. It's this whole revitalization project, where people can walk through the center of town without cars impeding their progress. So."

Leah nodded, understanding. "Right. Okay."

Now she understood why she hadn't actually seen a car since she'd parked in the lot.

"Good. Now we get down to business. How's it going

with Samuel?"

Leah sighed. Somehow 'getting down to business' always meant talking about Samuel.

Well.

Not always, but enough…at least in this context, where it did.

But all she said to her cousin as she headed down the block before stopping to get a tumbler of iced coffee was: "Yes. Samuel."

"How's it going?"

Telling Naomi the man was still on her mind and had been for at least three days was not happening. Instead she shrugged. "Still going."

Naomi nodded. "Interesting," her cousin said as she walked up to the window.

Leah braced herself as she watched Naomi buy an identical tumbler of iced coffee. "How so?"

"It's been a bit since you played his girlfriend at the expo and he played your boyfriend at the photo exhibit. You've gone with him to at least a gala and maybe the cocktail party your boss had. That's like a bunch of things."

"So?"

"Shayna's been running interference with everybody since before the gala, but everybody's starting to talk about the fact you're being around him willingly."

Which in Naomi's skeptical tone sounded like a mistake. Which it was not. And so she explained it as clearly as she could. "Things are going," she said. "It's nice. We're chatting. We've been in situations where we needed help or to bring a significant other. And we just, went with it."

She didn't need to know that there was a contract involved.

"I see," Naomi said. "And are there any other *obligations* you have on your calendar that will require you to *bring a significant other*?"

"I mean he's got a birthday party that's going to be thrown by his mentor," she replied. "And it's going well. I've gotten to know some of these people and...you know. They're nice."

"So why don't I feel like you're as all in on this as you seem to be?"

Leah shrugged, following her cousin down the street toward some of the benches they'd set up in front of what normally was a big bank of parking meters. "I mean," she said. "He's doing Judith's ketubah, and we've been hanging out. How more into this do you think I should be?"

Naomi took a long drink of her coffee. "I'm the last person in the world who should be judging this or you," she said. "But you need to figure out what you want from this relationship, and what you're willing to give."

Which was smart advice, but as they headed toward Liv and brunch, Leah tried to figure out what else she needed. Aside from a few more hours in the day to answer the questions she didn't have answers to, as well as deal with the fact that Samuel's voice sang in her head, there wasn't really anything.

AARON CALLED HIM on Sunday morning, and Samuel arrived at Aaron and Tommy's apartment for brunch before heading into Manhattan on a rare Sunday at the office.

"So what's up?" Samuel said as he sat down in front of Aaron's desk.

"Just taking stock," Aaron said. "Liam sent you the payment for the logo, so that's good. And you've got payments from a bunch of the commissions. Things are going well."

But from Aaron's tone, Samuel could tell there was a 'but' coming. "And?"

"There's a congregation in Virginia who want you to write a Sefer Torah."

That was it, wasn't it? The final frontier toward being a full-fledged sofer. He'd spent the last few years perfecting his craft, working on ketubahs, and then mezuzahs and finally a small congregation in Massachusetts had asked him to write them a megillah.

Right before the 'hot sofer' thing had started. Which ground all possibility for a Sefer Torah to a halt.

He was used to pivoting, changing his ideas and choices. He hadn't expected to be able to go back into lettering, but Liam had been there right when he needed, as the contacts for various lettering assignments came in. One from the Mitzvah Alliance, which led to the poster for the Goldstone Saga series.

And yet he didn't know how to react to this single pivot. "Wow."

Aaron looked at him; if he were in a comic panel, he'd have instructions to letter a rather large question mark over his brother's head. "What gives?"

He loved letters, loved writing them in different ways, but apparently he had the use of none of them in this situation. "I…uh…"

"Not that it matters," Aaron continued as if he hadn't said anything, "but I'd think you'd be a little more excited about this. Isn't this the last test you needed to pass through as a sofer?"

"It is."

"And what exactly is going on in your head?"

He didn't know how to answer; that was the problem. Words wove in and out of his head. None of them stuck, except the text he'd sent Leah that she hadn't responded to.

"Do you have any mysterious meetings this week?"

That he could answer. "Liam wants time with me this week," he said. "He made a big deal of it at the gala.

"I mean," Aaron said, the words sounding exactly as annoyed as the sigh heralded they would, "this is nothing new, Samuel. I can see you weighing your options and whatever mysterious whatever that you think Liam is about to throw your way stuck behind a barrier of stress and indecision. Because here's the thing. You have to decide."

Predictable as ever. Leah had correctly told him that he needed a poker face, but more importantly, he needed a response to his brother's inquiry. "I am deciding."

"Really?" Aaron said. "About what want to do with your life?"

"Yes?"

"Both personally and professionally, and by the agonized look on your face, I can tell that the last thing you want in this world is to do this Sefer Torah, the thing you've been working toward most of your professional life."

It was Samuel's turn to sigh, and run his hand through his hair in agony. "I don't know," he said. "I don't know what to say."

"No," Aaron said. "You know what the right words are. You're just afraid to use them."

"I don't want to disappoint Moreh, my teacher who spent years on someone who came from art school," he said, "or Mom and Dad or you..."

"Hiding behind disappointing people including your teacher, is not the bravery you think it is."

"I don't think it's bravery at all," Samuel said. "It's...I just want to make sure things run smoothly, you know?"

"Yes. Exactly. Because perfectionism is really the value you want to exhibit right now. But this is what you need to know."

"What?"

"You're not being brave or smart or loyal by stalling You're not giving people space by vehemently refusing to take up your own."

"But…"

"No buts, no wondering, no questions. Nothing. Because I'm trying to understand this."

"Okay," he said, as if his brother hadn't dropped enough on his shoulders. "What else are you trying to understand?"

"Leah. What does Leah think of any of this?"

He blinked. The very last thing he expected to discuss with his brother, here and now in the office, was the situation with Leah. "I'm confused. What do you mean?"

"Let's not beat around the bush. At all. You didn't just reach for the random person to play your girlfriend at the expo. You want her back, right?"

"I don't want to ask for miracles."

"What?" Aaron glared at him, and Samuel felt the exasperation come off his brother in waves. "Miracles?"

He nodded. "Miracles. We're getting to know each other again," he said, staying as close to the line as possible. "And I think more than that is a miracle, even though, yes, that is what I want."

The expression on Aaron's face went from exasperation to disappointment in two seconds flat. The sigh went internal as opposed to the gusty outside sigh, and the muscles that had tensed loosened, as if there wasn't any more fight in his brother.

"What?"

Aaron shook his head. "I just don't get you."

Which was a far deeper comment than he was prepared to handle. But all the same, he was there, with his brother. So he went for it; rather, he allowed the door to open. "I guess we're having this conversation?"

"You clearly haven't told her about what's happening with you," Aaron replied, running right past whatever conversation Samuel thought they were going to have into some kind of interrogation or something else of that nature. "You've probably introduced her to a bunch of people, and let her dance through your professional life like you do, without the actual work of all of it, right?"

"I'm not following," he managed.

"The expo, comic con. The gala. You're doing professional things, but she's a brilliant person. Do you trust her with your professional dilemmas? Do you trust her with any of your dilemmas?"

"I trust her," he said. "I do, But she's a really busy person who doesn't have time to deal with her own stuff, let alone my dilemmas."

"My God," Aaron said, his voice cutting through the thoughts that raged in Samuel's brain. "Samuel. You're refusing to reach for what you want, and your insistence of shoving yourself down in front of her makes it look like you don't trust her. You nincompoop."

"I'm not a nincompoop."

"I'm your brother," Aaron said. "I'm the official department in charge of determining that you are, in fact, a nincompoop. Because the way you're acting is going to cost you."

"I don't want to make the wrong decision, and I don't want to make her feel like it's her responsibility to solve my problems."

"Well, there are many things wrong with that statement," Aaron said. "We'd be here all day and miss the fun things we had planned if I went through all of them. But don't ever wait till things are perfect to share, because people might thing you're either hiding something, or that you don't trust them, okay?"

As he sat, letting Aaron's words digest before heading out on the family outing to the Manhattan Museum of Jewish History, aka the MMJH, Samuel tried to figure out what to do. More importantly, what he wanted to do.

WHEN SHE GOT back from Briarwood, in the privacy of her own apartment, whether it was because the sound of his voice ringing in her head was driving her up the wall, or because she couldn't help herself, she texted Samuel.

Except she didn't want to stop texting him. Granted it was late and it was possible he was heading to bed, and would drop off a potential conversation easily and quickly, she got into bed, plugged in her phone and texted him. *Good day? Bad day?*

There wasn't a very long pause before there was a reply.

Family outing, so good day, laundry and cleaning filled night. You?

She laughed as she texted him back. *Same. Taking care of the aftermath of a family day back in the suburbs.*

My sympathies.

She laughed. *Not as bad as all that. Liv was overseeing something and everybody else came along for the ride.*

There was a familiarity with talking to Samuel that she appreciated, even though she didn't want to start examining why, or understanding it.

Aaah. Aaron and Tommy wanted to go museum hopping, so I came along for the ride.

Which sounded very similar, if she translated what she knew of Samuel's family, to her own outing. *Sounds good.*

It was a nice exhibit at the MMJH. You'd like it.

We should go.

She found herself sitting there, wanting to take the text back, and thinking she'd made a mistake in sending it. She wondered if she could unsend it, and hoped he'd gone to bed, closed his eyes. But right as she was about to put the phone on her night table and go to bed, the light started blinking again.

Looking forward to it. Goodnight.

Except now sleeping was an impossibility, as her heart was pounding way too hard against her chest for her to breathe.

Chapter Nineteen

SAMUEL FOUND IT difficult to focus on work after he'd texted with Leah.

We should go.

Leah wanted to go somewhere with him outside the contracted set of events.

Whoa.

Was forgiveness within his grasp? Was a conversation with her about their future within his grasp?

Was a real future with her within his grasp?

He didn't know. What he did know was that Liam's party was coming up and he was getting to the end of their scheduled events, which meant renegotiation and a conversation.

He hoped.

As he started to try and focus on the list of commissions, his phone buzzed. It was Liam.

"Hey," he said when he answered the call. "How can I help you?"

"Do you have time for me? I have a work project to talk to you about."

And of course, for Liam, work meant BP, aka Banana-Pants.

When he'd first gone to art school, Samuel had dreamed, like every single person in his major, to go to work for one of the big companies, the ones whose comics he'd read as a kid. And like his father, Samuel's big comic obsession was BP. His life path had gone differently when he fell in love with alphabets and lettering styles that even the Jewish-founded BP would never ever want to put in the middle of a comic book.

But all he could manage to tell his mentor was: "Absolutely."

"Good," Liam said. "I'm in an office space. And take a breath, man. You're ready. You knew this was coming."

Samuel did but, in all fairness, hearing Liam talk about how he'd been preparing him for bigger things was different than actually being told by his mentor that those things had arrived.

Thoughts ran through his head as Samuel got on the subway and headed to the Manhattan address.

Liam was waiting downstairs. "Come on up," he said.

He passed the posters, the statues and the promotional models—the things that made it clear this was a BP-owned building. The history in this building was making his head spin faster than it already was.

"Take a breath," Liam said as they got off the elevator and headed toward what looked like Liam's office. "Sit down, have a soda."

Taking the advice, and the soda, Samuel settled down in the chair in front of Liam's desk. "I'm here," he managed.

"You are," Liam replied.

He could feel his feet in his sneakers on the ground, his jeans on the chair seat, his back against the comfortable chair back. Grounding himself.

"I have a project for you. But first you get background."

Samuel nodded. "I'm all ears."

Liam nodded, grabbed a folder. "So before I start, you need to know that this conversation didn't happen if you don't want to do this. There will be NDAs signed before the project is revealed."

He knew that; it was part and parcel of doing business. And that made things difficult most of the time, but it was important. "Go ahead," he said. "I'm excited."

"So for the last few years, people have been asking about a different angle for one of our properties after a certain MoviePix property you might know did well."

"I assume you're talking about Goldstone?"

The Goldstone Saga, Melanie Gould writing as MG Emerson's series of historical romances about a British-Jewish family turned television juggernaut. The work he'd done for it had changed the course of Samuel's career, making him believe that there was a place for him in more mainstream lettering.

But what made Samuel think, was that the lead actor in

the adaptation was Sam Moskowitz. Amongst other things, Sam Moskowitz was famous for playing the character of Mr. Shadow in the recent movie adaptations of the Shadow Squad comics.

Was this for the oft-discussed Mr. Shadow's origin series?

Liam nodded, either oblivious to or ignoring the strange expressions that had to accompanied the random thoughts in Samuel's head.

"But yeah. Goldstone changed a great deal, or at least opened a few doors. Which meant that suddenly this new angle on an old property was feasible. We tested it out in comic form first, and it did really well."

Yep. Samuel was convinced, this was going to be Mr. Shadow; he'd seen the comics and the stories that surrounded them. Especially considering the comics were put together by an all-Jewish team. He felt like he was going to fly off the chair, but he held himself back. "This sounds good."

Liam snorted. "You need a poker face," he said. "Because I can see the deductions and problem-solving running through your head as if I were inside it."

"Sorry," Samuel said, suitably chastened and embarrassed all at the same time.

"You can't bottle your enthusiasm," Liam said. "You're excited about this, and no I'm not confirming or denying until you sign. Anyway, back to the story. The comics sold so well, the decision was made to move the project from comics into a limited series format."

Unlike some of the other companies, BP hadn't started playing with television yet. Which meant this was even bigger news. "Television?"

"Yep. Poker face," Liam said as Samuel found himself laughing again.

"Sorry."

"No worries. Anyway the company's been looking for a way to experiment, if you will. And this is it."

Which was fascinating.

So the Mr. Shadow origin series was going to be BP's first foray into television.

Fascinating.

So many questions ran through Samuel's mind, one of the many being whether Sam Moskowitz was going to be involved.

"Wow. This is fantastic."

"Again," Liam replied, grinning, neither confirming nor denying. "But yes. It is."

"So…" Samuel managed. "What part do you want me to play?"

"That's easy," Liam replied. "We want to do a series of custom posters to tie the comics into the television series, taking it from the first series to the starting point of the new one."

Which was something that Samuel had never expected. Lettering for BP in this way. But all he managed was: "Story art in poster form? That's wonderful. A collectible series?"

"That's the idea. And we're hoping for an all-Jewish team to pull this off. Jewish writers got the concept, a Jewish artist doing main; heck I lured Oliver back to do colors."

"Oh wow," Samuel managed, feeling and sounding like a broken record.

"Right, it's exciting stuff," Liam said. But then he paused, and the expression on his mentor's face made him feel as if something huge was about to happen.

"But here's the thing. To do this right, we need a good, strong Jewish letterer."

And there it was. The payoff, not exactly the offer but enough of one at this point, with all of this information and an NDA possibility, it felt like an implied offer, if not a full one.

All the same, Samuel couldn't contain his excitement. "Oh wooow," he said, knowing *in fact*, that he'd become a broken record.

"There's a catch though," Liam said, as if he'd sensed Samuel's eagerness. Then again, Samuel figured it was pretty obvious how attractive this idea, even in theory, was. "So you have to think about this."

"Thinking," he said with a smile. "But I need to know what the catch is before thinking further."

"See this is special. We...want to lean in to the idea of making this series, this poster, a commitment to Jewish fans, bits of Easter eggs tied to Jewish culture..."

"Afikomen, you mean. Not Easter eggs."

"Right," Liam said with a smile. "Can't be Easter eggs if we're talking Jewish content. Yes, a-fi-KO-men. Right. Anyway. So one of the things we want is the kind of lettering that's traditional. The stuff you do when you're not working on posters."

"You mean," Samuel said as if he needed to double-check the words coming out of Liam's mouth, "you want me to mix and match and incorporate microcalligraphy, for example, with comic lettering?"

"Yes. Exactly. We want these posters to scream 'we're not playing'—show that Jewish content, this story and these characters mean something to us. Which is why we'd need you. You in?"

He wanted to say yes immediately, on the spot. Wasn't this the culmination of his work up until now?

The training on both sides—the lettering and the sofer-ing (if that was even a word?)

It felt almost too good to be true.

Except he'd been around the industry—creative industries in general—long enough to know that projects like this one always, without fail, were not only complex, but also came with strings, no matter how clear the ideas seemed at the outset There were schedules and the workload of his other projects and commitments to take into account.

Including the offer from Virginia of the Sefer Torah.

Which he had to respond to in some fashion, and soon.

But Liam didn't need to know that. What he did need to

hear was more concrete. "When do I need to make my decision?"

"Think about it. I've got to do a bit more finessing on this end to get all the loose ends tied up. When I get that done, I'll call you and we'll talk more about things. But more importantly, you'll be at the party this week?"

Samuel nodded. "I will be."

"And you're bringing the girl you took to comic con?"

Samuel nodded. "Leah. Yes."

"Good. She's family. Don't mess it up."

Samuel laughed. "Funny thing. Trying to figure out how to fix it if I do?"

"All I know," Liam said with a laugh, "is that you have to be prepared to talk, to make yourself look silly to make her smile. Friend of mine walked around in the middle of his girl's hometown wearing a menorah on his head to convince her how serious he was."

"That is…"

"It's what she needed," Liam said. "I know someone else burned his fingers trying to make a necklace, let alone how he agonized over the engagement ring because his girl would *know* bad from good jewelry."

Samuel nodded. "Do what she likes. You mean? Learn her language?"

"That is exactly what I'm saying," Liam replied. "Don't tell her what I talked to you about. But everything else. You know."

He did. At least he hoped he did. He'd find out if he could manage it all without losing his mind as they approached the party.

Not to mention, it wasn't strange that the first person he wanted to talk to as soon as he got this news was her?

Was it?

Even though he couldn't be anything more than vague about it?

All the same, he wanted her to share his excitement, even if he couldn't exactly explain why he was excited.

LOOKING FORWARD TO it. Goodnight.

Leah's entire world had been changed by those six words.

At least that's how it felt.

Tangled threads looked braided, and she'd typed words that she could no longer take back.

Her head was spinning.

Misguided invitations and so many other things were going on.

Luckily, Thursday was an office day and there were things she needed to talk to Bruck about; unfortunately something she'd seen online that morning had reminded her how important it might be to have a crisis PR rep on call to deal with any issues that arose with the Empires once Carly made it clear she was trying to join the team.

As she was making her list, her desk phone beeped twice,

indicating the office intercom.

"Leah?"

"Hi, Bruck," she said after she picked up the receiver. "What's going on?"

"Can you come to my office? I need to talk to you about something."

She smiled. "On my way."

Thinking about timing and threads, her smile turned into a grin as she headed down the hall. "Hey," she said as she walked into his office, "you wanted to see me?"

"Yeah, I've got a few things to talk about," Bruck said.

She nodded, settled into the chair in front of his desk. "Whenever you're ready."

"Good. I like that you're prepared. Anyway, I heard back from my contact about the betting company?"

"Oh great," she said, taking the notes; athletes were getting more and more intertwined with betting companies and it was important to know the details no matter what she felt about them. "Thank you. I really appreciate it."

"Not a problem," he said. "Anything else on your mind?"

"I actually have another question," she said.

"Okay," he said. "Talk to me."

"I'm starting to play phone tag with my contact at the Empires about one of my clients. Long story short, there was a two-party contract, with the major party being public, but the minor party being private until such time as the client's ready. Client is ready and the minor party, which has always been the Empires, is going to take over."

"So Carly's ready?"

She wondered how she could have thought Bruck wasn't paying attention to her, her business or her clients. "Yes," she said. "Spoke to her a few days ago and she confirmed, so phone tag."

"Great," he said. "Oh I forgot to ask you about the gala. How was it?"

Of course, the gala had been on her mind…heavily. But Leah had a feeling her boss didn't want to hear about where her lips had been, or who she'd spent the night with and the day after texting.

Which meant she had to pull herself together. "Good," she finally said. "They did a great job; the speeches were wonderful."

"Glad to hear it. I wanted to go," he confessed, "but my wife had other plans. But anyway…so Carly told you she's ready. Glad the news hadn't gotten out."

"Oh," she said, smiling again. "Not our first time on this merry-go-round. We had the conversation in private, and you're the first person I've really discussed it with."

Bruck's nod of approval was everything.

But she couldn't let him know that, not when he was still considering her for partnership.

"That's good," he continued, as if he hadn't noticed her reaction. "Especially with news like this. Do you know what kind of PR they're going to do with this?"

"Well," she said. "Funny thing."

"Oh?"

"I wanted to see if I could add something in the contract about putting a crisis PR rep on call to handle whatever issues, whether social media or otherwise, come up. Do you have any thoughts on the matter, or do you have any ideas on people you think who can pull it off?"

"That is interesting," Bruck said. "Let me shake some trees, see if we have some contacts for that. But I like the idea. I think based on the situation, that asking for it should be a bare minimum request of them."

She nodded. "Yeah. There are a few other things, which I'll run by you later, but I wanted to get this out first."

"Good. What are you thinking about in regards to the deal? Terms?"

"One way, major only. You put her in the minor, and this, what she's going through to do it, I don't think, isn't worth it."

He shook his head. "You sure?"

"She would have made the team a few years ago, on an open tryout," Leah replied, her rationale clear in her head. Not to mention her confidence in Carly. "And yes, it's been a bit since she's worked out heavily enough, but it was less time between her finishing the Legends season and stopping for maternity leave than her injury and the tryout."

"Well," Bruck said. "It's a risk. It's definitely a risk. Then again, as you pointed out, dealing with what she's going to deal with to play is also a risk."

Leah nodded. "Not to mention her brother-in-law wants to play with her as an Empire before he retires."

"He does?" Bruck raised an eyebrow. "Is he pressuring her?"

Leah would have laughed, but family was family. And she knew how well that went; there was pressure and then there was…something else.

Which was when she realized she'd been avoiding her sister, but that was another story entirely.

"He's encouraging her," she said. "There are so many reasons stacked against her, but Chris is doing his best to remind her that there are reasons and people in her corner. Which is lovely."

"That is nice," Bruck said. "He'd be going to the media?"

"He doesn't want to make it a circus." She paused. "She's also going to change her name."

"She changing her name? Really?"

Leah nodded. "One of the things Chris has talked about, and it stuck in her head, was that a lot of the conversation in hockey are about hockey families. And as a gift or a surprise or whatever, and maybe an understanding? She's changing the name on the back of her jersey to Emerson when she plays for the Empires."

"I like that," Bruck said. "Give the Empires a bit of history. First brother and sister-in-law to play on the same team. Nice. Okay."

And as they continued to chat, Leah was excited.

And at the same time, she couldn't wait to tell Samuel.

Which was strange. But she'd go with it.

As long as she didn't text him.

SAMUEL FOUGHT THE battle against texting Leah for hours. He'd managed to succeed through dinner (random knishes ordered from Greenblatts) and a bunch of commission work.

Once again, he made a note to tell his brother how glad he'd been that the names of the people he was working for were left out of his notice. Because even though he wanted to know who he was doing these for, he was glad he didn't.

But eventually, he lost the battle and texted Leah.

How was your day? I got good news I can't share but I'm excited.

Which was a confusing message, he realized, but he hoped she'd get it. In some way, shape or form. And instead of pondering over what she was going to say, he put the phone down, within arm's reach of course, and went back to work.

Eventually, his phone buzzed, so he put his quill down and picked up the phone.

Leah.

Oooh. Good news?

He couldn't tell her. He wanted to. But he couldn't. So he settled for something that made sense, at least to him.

Good news I can't talk about.

He went back to the mezuzah, carefully inscribing the text onto the piece of parchment.

Eventually, his phone buzzed again.

Leah.

I'm confused.

So he wasn't as clear as he thought he'd been. Finally he decided on something else, something more specific that he hoped would make sense.

Industry things. It's good.

This time he held the phone, watching the dark circles dance in front of his eyes until they materialized into an answer.

I'm glad. It was a good day for me too.

Even better. Not just another request for clarification, but an actual conversation piece.

But the dots were still dancing in front of his eyes.

When's the party?

Which on a Monday night, made sense to ask. So he took a chance, hoping she'd go along with it.

Thursday. Come over to my apartment before?

Samuel's heart pounded in time with the moving dots as he waited for the answer. Would she tell him no? Would she agree? Would she…

Debrief? Maybe talk a bit?

He almost dropped the phone, most likely lost his mind for a moment, if nothing else lost the tether of string keeping him close to reality for as long as it took him to process what she'd texted.

She. Said. Yes.

Sounds good. See you Thursday.

And he sent the text before he did something silly, like ask if she wanted to plan the outing to the museum. Or maybe discuss the past.

ON TUESDAY, LEAH had to acknowledge that her head had been a full on mess since she'd texted with Samuel on Sunday night and sent that misguided invitation.

What had she been thinking?

It was bad when it was just 'let's go to the museum'—something she could have forgotten; heck, it was simply a thought bubble of an invitation that he didn't turn into reality.

But she had to make it worse on Monday night by saying that she'd love to debrief and talk before the party.

What the hell had she been thinking?

The problem, of course, was that she hadn't.

She'd been fantasizing about her fake boyfriend, at the worst of all times—when she should be prepping to talk to the contracts department at the Empires, playing phone tag for Carly.

Leah had to do something. Thankfully, Naomi had called, saying that Liv had tried on a few dresses at the shop in Crystal Harbor and was impressed, and could she come over.

Usually, bridesmaids dresses weren't her favorite way of spending time, but a mid-week break from the city was exactly what the doctor ordered; it got her away from a place where she'd be tempted to text Samuel, and keep her on her toes because she'd be around relatives.

Not to mention she liked the shop where she'd bought her dress for the gala; and Chava the tailor was lovely.

When she arrived, she saw that Shayna had come along to give Ramona a chance to try on some matching flower girl dresses.

"Is this the last bunch of dresses we're trying on?"

Naomi shrugged. "First bunch Liv tried on, so who knows."

"And," Shayna said with a laugh, "our little pint-sized fashion critic has opinions as well."

Leah nodded, considering the implications of Ramona's fashion sense. "As long as we don't look like look like cream puffs or Medusa or..."

"You're all right," Naomi said. "But Leah is closer to where we're going. Judith's the star and as long as the bridesmaids don't look like the gorgon sisters and Ramona doesn't out-glitter rainbow anybody, we'll be fine."

And as the parade of dresses began, Leah found herself thinking of Samuel, how it would feel to have him there with her, giving her opinions, maybe showing up unexpectedly there at the shop like he had the last time she was there, putting his hands on her shoulders, her waist...

"Leah?" Naomi's not so dulcet tones broke into her train of thought. "You're not here and we need you."

Leah shook her head before she realized her cousin couldn't see her through the dressing room door. "Sorry."

Which she was. Unfortunately, the break in her thought process forced her to acknowledge that she'd been fantasizing about her fake boyfriend again.

And that was dangerous.

Because as much as she wanted to tamp down her emotions, and if nothing else ignore them, they were intruding. Again.

Not only intruding, but bubbling up and exploding inside of her.

And that led to one inescapable conclusion.

Leah wanted the real deal.

She wanted an actual go of it with Samuel. A real, actual, real-life, adult-sized try with him.

And that terrified her to the point where she had to hold on to the wall of the dressing room.

Which made her finally ask the question that had been bugging her. "I wonder…how you know if it's real."

As soon as she verbalized the question, she remembered where she was. Not in her apartment or her office or anywhere else that guaranteed her a speck of privacy.

She was in a public dressing room and she'd expressed this ridiculous, impossible question to her cousin, with her sister-in-law somewhere nearby.

Which meant she had to pull it back.

And yet she knew very well that it was too late; you couldn't put toothpaste back into the tube and this wasn't something she couldn't just suck back into her mouth. At least she'd said it in the dressing room because otherwise she'd have ended up with her cousin, possibly her sister-in-law and possibly her little niece staring at her like pumpkins or Cheshire cats or whatever.

She got that anyway. Or at least she'd end up with the verbal equivalent.

"What?" Shayna, her eagle-eared sister-in-law, was the one who said something, her voice the equivalent of a hammer piercing something with a nail.

"Go change," Naomi said, sounding hurried and, as usual, focused on the task at hand, which was the dresses. "We'll talk about this later, because of course we really need to talk."

Which meant though Naomi was focused, she wasn't letting this go. Not at all.

And later did in fact come, after more dresses, and a moment where a little four-year-old who'd gotten a very glittery dress, was dropped off into the care of her father and brother.

A table, one large Cupcake Stop cupcake for each of them and her cousin and her sister-in-law were staring at her.

She'd ordered an americano, hoped it took forever to arrive, but that night, Cupcake Stop was faster than usual.

The drinks arrived, and left her no more time to stall.

And nobody was giving her a chance to breathe.

"What?"

"There's a story you need to tell," Shayna said. "Because you said you wanted to know how 'it' was real. The *it* I'm assuming you're talking about means love? Relationships, yes?"

Knowing she wasn't going to get out of this, Naomi nodded. "Yes."

"So what do you mean specifically?" Naomi asked. "What's the *it* you want to be real?"

Leah sighed, and admitted it: "Love."

"So," Naomi asked, "what you're asking is how do you know when love is real?"

Leah nodded, took a bite of her cupcake. "That's exactly what I said, but both of you should probably realize how much I actually want to discuss this, which is not at all."

"You're kidding," Shayna said with a snort. "Two things. We're family, and I've been running interference for you."

"Yes," Leah said. "I'm very aware and even more grateful, which is why, you know, I'm even talking in the first place."

"Good," Naomi said, "you're improving on this conversation thing."

"Right," Shayna said, continuing the conversation like it was her right. "So. You want to know when love is real. I mean, not to put too fine a point on it, you've been doing a pretty good job demonstrating it the last few weeks with

Samuel. I think you're doing just fine."

"Yeah," Naomi said. "You've been hot and heavy with Samuel since the photo exhibit."

And that was when she couldn't take the pressure of holding this secret back any longer, and the dam burst, words pouring out of her as if she were Niagara Falls. "It's fake."

That was when Naomi's jaw hit the table, but it was Shayna who spoke. "I am fascinated by this whole thing," she said. "You really went through the trouble of setting up a fake relationship?"

Leah nodded. "Yeah. We have a contract and everything."

Naomi shook her head. "When did this start? After the wedding expo and the photo exhibit?"

Shayna raised an eyebrow. "What was that?"

Leah took a sip of her hastily ordered espresso, and told the story of the wedding expo and explained what had happened at the photo exhibit that same night. "And then basically a bunch of things happened—invitations, circumstances, where it just made sense to…fake a relationship. And so he made us a contract. So yeah."

"Well," Shayna continued, "at least now we know why you were asking about the difference between real and fake. But my question is why exactly did you think fake dating would be a good idea?"

"It was convenient," she said. "Samuel was there, he

needed me, then I needed him, so we decided to use each other for a prescribed period of time and when it's over, things were supposed to end without a scar on either of us."

"I'm trying to find a place where you explain why you didn't tell me before, but we'll get to that later," Naomi said, making Leah feel guilty and nervous simultaneously. "For now, I want to know why Samuel was such a good choice."

Of course it was Naomi who got to the heart of the matter.

"Because we shouldn't be together," Leah finally said. "We were a horrible idea. I mean let's face it. In those movies, or books where couples fake-date, nine times out of ten, they don't know each other when they start. And these couples end up a fake fail because during the process of dating, they discover each other, even though they don't know the pitfalls of dating or even knowing this particular individual. So they learn the good parts *and...poof.* Real feelings come up. With Samuel, he was a bad idea, and I knew from the beginning exactly why he was a bad idea. There was supposed to be no poof. No reason why there should be real feelings."

Both Shayna and Naomi snickered in a way that made Leah uncomfortable.

"Right. So you did your research—read books and watched movies and TV shows about fake dating, and you decided that you'd outsmart the trope and be the exception," Shayna said. "Except here you are, asking your cousin and your sister-in-law if they can recognize real love."

"While you're trying on a bridesmaids dress, no less," Naomi said.

Adding insult to injury, was the fact that Leah had decided she was not going to poke at Naomi about Jason. Nope. She was going to be good. For good or evil, she'd brought this subject up in the first place, and she was going to be stuck with it. "Fine, fine," she said. "Poof might mean acknowledging real feelings, not just them existing."

"Because," Naomi added, "look at it this way. Feelings, emotions, love, are the complete opposite of rational. They show up when you least expect them or want them to. They're a mess."

Which made Leah sigh. "Fine," she said. "So I may have caught real feelings, and am in the process of having my *poof* moment."

"Which," Shayna said, "makes me think that all along, the real question you're asking is how you make this fake situation real. And that's with trust. You need to trust him *and* tell him how you're feeling."

"So," Naomi added, "what are you going to do about the fake fail moment you're having? Are you going to tell Samuel you want something real or...?"

"I'm supposed to see him in a few days," Leah said, addressing both her interrogators at once as she figured out how to answer their questions. "We're going to a birthday party."

Naomi said, "Which doesn't answer the question your sister-in-law, or I asked. And maybe that's something you need to think about?"

Leah sighed. Honesty was probably the best tactic she had at the moment, and though she didn't really want to admit her feelings, she was going to have to if she was hoping to survive this. "I don't know," she admitted, being as careful as she could. "I don't know if I want to actually do anything about the feelings. I almost lost my mind when I texted him about going with him to the MMJH. We're not a good idea and yet I can't handle this..."

"Can you please listen to yourself?" Liv asked. "You have these ideas about him because of who you were and who he was back in high school. Both of you have changed since then. Both of you are different people."

She found herself remembering the conversation she'd witnessed him having with Josephine Bruck. Maybe he had changed, found his voice enough to use it on behalf of people he cared about?

"Maybe?"

Shayna shook her head; apparently her sister-in-law had morphed into some wizened expert. "You're way past maybe. Heck; you're already talking about including him in things."

Which was true. She'd never send a text like that if she wasn't in some way ready to talk about the past, her feelings and making her fake relationship real. Even with all of its...foibles and treachery.

And that led her to one inexorable conclusion. "You're right," she told her sister-in-law.

"Excellent." And after Naomi left to head back to Manhattan, Shayna grinned at her. "I will," Shayna said, "at some point expect to see him at Shabbas dinner or dessert or something later. Because I can't keep you insulated from the family gossip forever."

"It's something we planned for," Leah said. "But I promise you'll be the first to know when I schedule it."

"*When*," Shayna said, grinning. "I like the sound of those words. And that would make sense, considering we're hosting your family Shabbat."

As she headed back to Manhattan, Leah started to think about Samuel and about their situation. Did she have the words to actually talk about what had happened all those years ago? Was she actually capable of seeing the incident through the eyes of adults looking at something under hermetically sealed glass?

She wasn't sure yet, but one thing she did know, was that she was going to see if she had the right words to initiate the conversation about the past so they could move forward. Because even if she wasn't yet ready, she needed to be ready soon.

Her heart, and what it wanted, depended on it.

Chapter Twenty

SAMUEL NEEDED TO calm down.

He needed to breathe, not sweat through his palms all over his jeans. And he wasn't sure what was going to happen.

His apartment was clean, he was ready to go and he had the birthday present ready and waiting.

He couldn't concentrate on the list of work he had to do. So he checked something off the list that was pending; sent the email to the congregation in Virginia, declining the opportunity to write the Sefer Torah due to other pending commitments, but that he'd love to be considered for future work.

And if that closed a door for him, he was okay with it.

Because he was happy with what he did—mezuzahs, megillahs, ketubahs and the occasional poster and the possibility of working with other creatives even if Liam's offer didn't officially come in.

Over the past few weeks, he'd collaborated with a bunch of people and done some fun things. Seen his lettering on large signs hung from buildings, on hockey masks and met some fascinating people.

And he'd been able to share all of these things with Leah.

Something he never thought he'd be able to do.

And yet there he was, out of his mind and thrilled. Even more so when Leah arrived at his apartment.

And she did. Jeans that fit her curves, a top that matched her eyes and a pair of sneakers that sparkled and matched her shirt.

He was more than just thrilled; he was mesmerized. "Hi," he managed. "You look gorgeous."

"Hi, yourself," she said as she came in, oddly awkward, oddly adorable. He hadn't seen this Leah in a long time and he wondered what it meant.

"Do you want to come in?" he asked, as if it was an option. It was barely an option but it broke the ice, gave them space.

She nodded. "Thank you," she said. And then shook her head. "This is awkward, isn't it?"

He laughed. "Yeah. It kinda is. But we've been through awkward before."

She nodded, and this time she didn't bristle at the merest mention of their past.

What did that mean?

As the silence between them stretched, he realized he was going to have to speak, or nobody was.

Which was different.

"What's going on?"

She shrugged, and he wasn't sure what territory they'd entered, because they clearly had embarked on some new phase of their interactions. Because she hadn't taken steps to hide her emotions yet like she usually did when she seemed remotely vulnerable.

He didn't know what to say either; nothing that came to mind could fall anything other than flat.

"Thinking about a bunch of things. You know?"

He nodded. He did, in fact, know about what a bunch of things rolling around in his mind actually meant. Especially since he'd taken care of one earlier in the day. But she didn't need to know that. Not yet. "I do know." He paused. "Do you want a drink?

"How much time do we have before we go?"

He checked his watch. "Not long," he said.

She looked down, looked anywhere but at him. Still letting her emotions and her vulnerability show.

"Do we have time to talk?"

He swallowed. "We don't have much time. But of course. About?"

"Can we talk about amendments or extensions or…"

She'd fought against extensions. Now she was asking about it? Victory. Vulnerability.

His heart pounded "Or?"

The moment extended, as if they were on a precipice, about to go somewhere new and better.

But the tension. The silence.

And then Leah swallowed. "High school."

It was a wonder he could stand; the words were soft, yet unmistakable.

He heard her. She'd said it.

She wanted to…

Talk about the past, the one thing she'd always said she couldn't do.

And yet.

And yet he had to go. To Liam's party, to the celebration of the potential offer being extended. To celebrate his friend's birthday.

And as Liam had put it: family.

But the alarm he'd painstakingly set so that they wouldn't be late? That's when it went off.

Of course it did.

"Table the discussion?"

She nodded. "After the party? Tonight? You and me? We talk?"

He smiled. "I'd like that."

The smile on her face was open, clear and beautiful. Making him feel as if on a Thursday night in Queens, they'd started anew.

So he took her hand and walked out of his apartment and into the future.

LEAH'S HEART WAS pounding as she walked with Samuel, hand in hand from the subway to the location of the party.

The rest of the week had been horrible; playing phone tag with the Empires about this contract provision and actually negotiating the contract that would be Carly's first with them was, to put it simply, a nightmare.

Phone tag, email tag, conversations.

There was so much to do, so much to unravel, and if she didn't love her job, it would be horrible. But Carly would be a trailblazer, and this contract had to be special.

But she still wanted this precious time with him; she'd carved it out of her schedule and told everybody she'd been speaking to that they shouldn't call unless it was an emergency.

Not just because she'd committed to this event contractually, but because she wanted to spend time with Samuel. To have the conversation she'd been practicing.

About high school.

About...chances and wanting more and just being together.

And all the worries about whether it was the right decision or not evaporated as she arrived at his apartment. The strong smell of ink enveloped her and instead of making her feel anxious, it made her feel at home.

And brought her right into the chocolate pools of his eyes.

She'd decided; she wanted to fix the past, and if she

could do that, she could grab for a future.

With him.

And yet as she stood there, holding his hand, all she could think of was how similar the stairs looked to the stairs that led up to Gabriel Bruckner's townhouse. The parallels between that night and this one were smacking her in the face. Hard.

The beginning and the next chapter, both starting in work parties.

"Is it me," she said, "or are you staring at the stairs too?"

"It's not you," he said. "And I am. It's funny, you know? I've been here before and yet I didn't notice the stairs before."

"Really?"

They were…rather large and would be out of place in any other type of residence here. But they fit."

Still noticeable.

"I notice them," she said, trying to pull her thoughts together, "because here I am, standing next to you, about to go up similar stairs into another party. So much has changed since then."

"You barely walked into my apartment the last time," he said. "We met in my brother's office space."

Which was true, but Samuel's delivery, in those gorgeous jeans and a shirt that showed off his forearms, made her want to laugh her butt off. "Yeah," she said. "Times change, people change."

She laughed, but a quiet laugh, one that made him smile.

She could get lost in that smile for hours, if not days.

Years if she was lucky…

But she didn't want to get ahead of herself.

She needed to get through tonight without any emergencies first.

"They do." he said. And then he looked at her, not just a normal Samuel smiling look, but something else.

Something deeper.

She couldn't look away if she wanted to.

"You ready?" he asked.

His voice popped her bubble, reminding her that this was an official appearance, a birthday party. He needed to impress people. Which meant she had to pull herself back from the pink fluffy clouds of emotion that were threatening to drown her.

"Yes," she said. "I'm ready. You?"

He nodded. "I am."

And knowing she couldn't do anything else, or say anything else, she trusted him to lead her upstairs and into a townhouse full of people he knew, her fingers brushing his with every step.

SAMUEL COULD NOT believe himself or his circumstances.

There he was, standing at the top of Liam's stairs, on a beautiful summer night in Queens, with Leah.

And they were about to go into the townhouse to celebrate Oliver's birthday.

Which if he'd been asked three years ago what the most significant part of the night, having decided that Leah was no longer someone who could be in his life, he'd answer the fact he'd be going to Oliver Goldsmith's birthday party.

But now, not only was he going to celebrate his friend and *collaborator* Oliver's birthday, he was taking Leah.

Life took him in interesting directions, in mysterious ways and paths he'd never understand. But here he was.

Here they were. "Here we go," he said when he dropped her fingers to knock on the door.

"Here we go," she said, as she took his hand back, the warmth of her hand welcoming on a night like this, as the scraping metal and the rattling chain followed by the creaking noise heralded the open door.

This was it.

Because the door revealed…Liam… Grinning like a fool. "Mr. Levine, welcome, welcome. Come in, come in," Liam said, making Samuel grin.

"Thank you for having us."

"Not a problem," he said. "You're family after all."

Which made Samuel feel warm inside, especially knowing that Leah was standing next to him.

"You too," Liam said, having turned toward Leah. "Glad we get to really chat in a comfy place like this one."

"I'm glad I was able to make it," she said, making Samuel smile.

"Good, good," Liam continued, still in host mode as he met Samuel's eyes. Yep. His mentor was in his element. "Anyway, not a big gathering tonight, unlike what we'd planned. But that's okay. A handful of artists and a good game of Pictionary with the non-dominant hand."

Leah laughed, and that laugh made Samuel feel on top of the world. "Pictionary?"

Liam turned to Leah, and Samuel wondered what he was going to say; the games were legendary and he was actually really excited that she was going to play with him for the first time.

"Yep. Knock-down drag-out games of competitive drawing, so wild that we had to institute the non-dominant-hand rule," Liam said. "So we continue, less alcohol, more fun. More drawing. More friends. More family."

"Looking forward to it," she said.

"And of course, I hope you're hungry," Liam continued. "Because you're not coming to my house without being fed. My family would never forgive me, let alone what the birthday boy would do."

Leah nodded. "I'm hungry."

"Good."

And as they headed inside, Samuel took her hand again.

"This is going to be nice," she said, and in her tone, he heard so much. It wasn't just nice, it was going to be fun and the beginning of their next chapter in ways that he hadn't been ready to contemplate before.

Chapter Twenty-One

EVEN THOUGH THE townhouse looked to Leah like Gabriel Brucker's from the outside, the inside was completely different. This wasn't cool and modern, but warm and colorful. Like a collection of comic artists had made the walls their playground.

Adding on to the effect, each room seemed to be filled with art in a way that just matched. Colors and sculptures and photographs, books and other random pieces were all over the space, and plastic figures lined some of the walls. Leah wasn't quite sure what to make of it, but she'd spent most of her life shoving herself into spaces she was unsure of. This was no exception.

The party space itself was great: two divided sets of couches, with an easel in the middle, with wide-open wooden doors that led to a dining table set family style, huge plates at the center.

This was going to be interesting. And she was so glad she'd come. "Those sneakers are killer."

Leah turned around only to see a young woman in front of her. The woman's jewelry was gorgeous as was her smile.

"Thank you," Leah replied, grinning. "I don't get a chance to wear them often, but I figured this group would appreciate it."

"Jamie Sawyer," she said. "My husband's on the other side of the room, refusing to wear the crown I bought him on principle."

This was the birthday boy's wife. Got it.

"Leah Nachman," she said, extending a hand. "Nice to meet you."

"Nice to meet you too," Jamie replied, thankfully shaking the hand Leah offered. "Who are you with?"

"Samuel," she said. "Liam is his mentor. He worked on the logo for Tzedakah Exchange?"

"Oh my God, Jamie," interrupted another voice. "That is the worst question you could possibly ask. I mean the first real date I had with Isaac was at Liam's actual birthday party that Isaac threw at his place. She could be with nobody, someone who's a crafter or artist in her own right, or with someone for the first time." And then the woman paused, shook her head. "Sorry. I have neither tact nor manners. I'm Sarah Lieberman. I…"

Sarah Lieberman.

Lieberman rang a bell.

Who was she…? Why did the name ring a bell?

"Leah Nachman," she said, deciding introductions would be better than thinking she'd dive into connections.

"Leah. Wait."

Yep. The curly-haired Sarah knew someone. Maybe Judith, maybe her brother? Liv?

"The name Nachman sounds familiar," Sarah continued. "Are you related to the Judith who saved Tony Liu's life?"

And there it was. This woman knew the inside story of what happened when Judith had been working as a departmental assistant at the Wall Street firm. Which means she could know anybody, but Leah would put her money on her knowing Judith's boss.

Either way, whoever she was, the woman had asked a question that deserved an answer. "That's my sister. I have a little less to recommend myself with."

"Interesting," Sarah said. "And the guy?"

"I've known him forever," Leah replied, deciding honesty was the best policy when this woman was already worried she'd stepped over a boundary or two, "but this is actually really only our...third date, so it's fine? Really."

Which wasn't accurate, but would do; these people weren't keeping score.

Were they?

That's so cool," Jamie said.

"Very," Sarah replied. "Liam told Isaac that there's a guy here tonight who did posters for my favorite author's series and my ketubah, and he's here. And I'm going to meet him."

"Just want to make sure," Leah said. "What series is that again?"

"Well," Sarah said after a bit. "She's my second favorite

author really. Melanie Gould's series, the Goldstone Saga?"

"That's Samuel," Leah confirmed. "He's the one who did the posters for the series. And he's also doing my sister's ketubah."

"Extremely small world."

Leah nodded, excited to speak to these women a little more, glad to find people within Samuel's circle she could talk to. So she followed Jamie and Sarah across the room toward the bar area. She took the cup Sarah gave her and reached for a pitcher marked Shirley Temples. As she lifted the pitcher, she poured herself a drink, making sure there was enough ice. "You want anything?"

Sarah, at that point, was standing in front of her, holding a glass filled with something blue. "A Pictionary partner who isn't going to drive me nuts? Maybe?"

They clinked glasses and Leah smiled.

"I don't draw but I'll do my best."

"That is all I can ask for," Sarah said.

Which made Leah even more excited.

She was going to be able to find friends in his friend group, which was important for many reasons she didn't want to think about. And so many that she did.

SAMUEL FOLLOWED LIAM through the house in awe. He barely recognized the place where he'd come a few times already to play cards.

"This setup is amazing."

"Friend of mine set it up," Liam said, shrugging, slightly embarrassed. "Best use of space is what he said—some kind of flow and design stuff. I don't get it. But how goes it so far?"

"Getting the lay of the land," he said. "Seeing who's here."

"I told you *a small group*," he said with a smile. "Your girlfriend's already making friends with Sarah and Jamie."

"I'm glad," he said. Because seeing her grow roots within his friend group made him feel things. "Worried about losing in Pictionary but if it's for the greater good, you know?"

"Yep," Liam replied. "Oh I get it. Ties. Threads, connections are so much easier that way."

Threads. Threads tying him and Leah closer together, roots of things and ideas. "Very much so," was what he said to Liam. Is there any big…plan?"

Liam laughed. "I take it you meant something about the birthday-related festivities?"

He nodded. "Yeah. Is there…some kind of schedule?"

"We're not doing cake because Oliver refused birthday trappings."

Samuel raised an eyebrow. "Is that usual?"

"For Oliver? Possibly. Attention isn't his thing, so we're just hanging out like a normal average everyday group of people having a party. Dinner first, then Pictionary."

"With Isaac Lieberman casually sitting in the corner?"

"He does that," Liam said. "But we all have our moments. But also, happy birthday, Oliver."

"Happy birthday," he said as Oliver joined him.

Oliver, the birthday boy, grinned. "Thank you. Thanks for coming."

"Dinner soon," Liam interjected, taking over the conversation as the host would be expected, "then Pictionary?"

Oliver nodded. "I think we're going to go down in Pictionary."

Liam raised an eyebrow. "What do you mean *we*?"

And of course that was when Samuel felt both Oliver's and Liam's eyes on him. "Uh…"

"You can write…"

"Writing isn't drawing," Samuel said "I'm not good at drawing. I'm horrible at it."

"But you're reeeeally good at writing…"

"I'm not ambidextrous either," he admitted.

This was going to be interesting. And he looked forward to every second of it.

LEAH'S STOMACH WAS about as full as her heart; the food Liam had served was amazing: pasta, meatballs, barbecue ribs he bought from the restaurant who catered Judith's Bat

Mitzvah, and the inevitable Greenblatt's Knishes.

"You having a good time?"

She smiled. Samuel had come up to join her as they left the dining room. She'd been sitting and chatting with Jamie and Sarah, strategizing for the game in ways that she hadn't prepared for and yet was thrilled about.

"I am," she said. "Thank you."

"For?"

He raised an eyebrow, but she understood. "This is fun, and I realized I'd said I would go, but I'm glad you said you'd bring me."

His smile built a warm fire in her stomach. "I'm glad you're here," he said. "Dinner was good?"

She nodded, stepping closer as he put his arms around her. "Yeah. Really good. You ate?"

"Mmmhm." He laughed. "I thought of you when I saw the Greenblatts box."

She snorted. "So many Greenblatts in my life, I cannot get away from them." And then she looked up into those eyes of his. "They were my comfort food."

"Now you know the inside scoop?" He paused, and she knew whatever he was going to say would be funny. "Or whatever you call the behind the scenes in knish world."

The laugh arrived out of nowhere even though she expected humor. The force of giddy joy exiting her mouth sent her forehead to his shoulder. "I don't know why it was so funny," she said once she'd calmed down enough to lift her head and look up into his eyes.

"The delivery," he replied. "Dry as old parchment."

"Probably." She paused and took a chance, following a random thread of conversation in her head, an idea she hadn't expected to want. "Do you want to get out of here or…?"

Of course, she'd known the second she got the question out of her mouth that for him, leaving wasn't going to be an option. This was professional networking as well as personal friend circle, and Pictionary was the highlight of the evening, it seemed, a long-standing tradition he'd clearly never been invited to.

Except it said something about her that she needed to ask him to leave, creating if not acknowledging yet another of the tangled, tied threads pulling on her and toward him.

To his credit, he didn't say no immediately; the fact that the power of her request was enough to consider it for even a second meant more to her than she could articulate.

Because, quite simply, she couldn't offer the same to him. When her work called, she couldn't say no. There were people depending on her to fix the problem that had come up when she got the call. People's livelihoods were on the line when she got the call. And she always needed to answer.

"I need to play," he finally said, his response both inevitable and predictable. But the strain in his eyes was not.

Did he think she was uncomfortable? Did he think she wasn't enjoying herself as much as she'd said?

"I know..." he began, the words slowly emerging from his lips. "I know you're making plans to play too? Are you?"

She nodded. "I am," she said. "A team with Sarah and Jamie—we'll see how that goes. I don't think any of us can draw."

He laughed. "I think that's the fun of this, maybe?"

She nodded.

"Maybe we can go after the game?"

"Sounds good," she replied. Even though he held her, then took her hand as they headed to the area where the game was set up, there was something in the back of her mind that worried her.

Things couldn't be this good, could they?

She wasn't sure, but she figured the best thing she could do was to follow along and enjoy it.

SAMUEL WAS BEYOND thrilled. He was sitting with his mentor, professional contacts and friends. He had a seat at the legendary Pictionary game, something he'd hoped for a long time he'd get to do.

And to add icing on the cake, Leah was sitting across the way from him, sending him grins and having a grand old time of her own.

The only thing was that he wished she was closer, on his team, going back and forth with him, guessing together.

But she'd already been claimed before he sat down, which meant he was sitting between Oliver and Liam.

If he'd been asked six months before if there had been anything that he'd wanted more than sitting next to Liam and Oliver at a Pictionary game, he say there'd be nothing.

Okay. Even then, in the back of his mind, in his wildest dreams, he never would have thought this scenario was possible.

And yet, now, here he was, living it.

He gazed across the room at Leah, meeting her gorgeous blue eyes with his own, watching as the grin on her face came to life, the wink following it, making promises he was excited to keep.

"You have a good one," Liam said with a smile.

"I do," he agreed.

And in the silence that followed, he heard a buzzing noise. "You have bees?"

Liam shook his head. "Nope. That's *Buzzus phonus*, not any bees we know."

Samuel nodded, before turning in the direction of the noise, only to stop at the expression on Leah's face. She was biting her lip, and the seconds passed before he realized what was going on.

The buzzing noise had been Leah's phone. And someone was trying to get in touch with her.

Insistently. Because the phone would stop, and then start again.

She sighed, then looked at him.

She looked helpless, and so Samuel nodded, whether she needed his encouragement or not.

Because the pattern had been repeated at least three times.

As if the nod from him was the okay she needed, Leah reached into her pocket, pulling out the device as it started buzzing again.

There was something in her expression as she turned, something that felt like an inevitability. He felt the tug on the thread between them, and he wondered what was going to happen as he watched her pull her phone from her pocket, glancing quickly at it.

Time stopped as he waited, wondering what she saw on the screen, what she needed, from him, what he had to do.

Instead of joy and relief, the surprise and annoyance in her expression as she turned back toward him told a different story. "I'm getting a call in about two minutes that I need to take," she said.

There was resignation and upset in her voice, as if she also felt the pressure on the thread between them. He nodded, turning to Liam. "Is there somewhere she can be private?"

Liam nodded. "Office is down the hall to the left. Look for the original art Shadow Squad poster on the wall," he said, gesturing at Leah.

She stood and headed down the hall, making his heart

clench.

He hoped everything was okay. More specifically, and more importantly, he hoped she was going to be okay. After dealing with whatever this was.

"Relax," Oliver said. "Whatever it is, you'll deal with it."

He nodded. "Right," he said.

"Right now," Oliver continued, "focus on the game. She'll tell you what she needs when she's done."

Considering Oliver was happily married to a woman with a demanding creative career of her own, Samuel nodded, taking the advice. He'd be there for Leah when she was ready to talk.

LEAH FOLLOWED THE directions Liam had given her and walked down the hallway, turning into the room just to the right of the large Shadow Squad poster.

She was struck with the inevitability of the situation. The second she found herself relaxed in the moment with Samuel, believing that a future was possible, the Empires called.

She'd never been so upset to receive a work call in her life.

She'd never been so upset to be right in her life, but the foreboding held her close.

She walked into the room, turned on the light and sat down on the closest chair.

"Leah," said the gentleman she'd been trying to get in touch with for the last week, "we need to talk. And we need to do it privately and quickly before the news gets out."

This was unconventional, but this was Carly.

They needed an iron-clad contract before the world found out that the mystery team in the deal Carly signed a few years before were the Empires. Before the world found out that the Empires were officially signing a woman to an MHL contract. The kind of contract that would guarantee a woman would actually see minutes in net during an MHL game.

Five years ago, this decision would be easy. Five years ago, she'd leave without a second thought.

Now, she was leaving, and she knew why she was leaving. But now? Now she also knew what she was leaving behind.

More specifically, not just what, but who.

"Send a car," she finally said. "Send a car to my location."

"Will do," the gentleman replied.

And as he ended the call, Leah headed out of the room and toward her fate.

With every step she took, Leah began the process of locking her emotions away; the very last thing she wanted was to let Samuel see how badly leaving was shaking her. She didn't want him to offer to come with her or something ridiculous like that.

This was work, not the occasion for a romantic rendezvous.

Leah didn't have the space in her life to devote to a real romantic relationship of any sort as it was. She'd finish Carly's contract and then end the relationship and the contract.

"What's up?" he said as she walked toward the group.

"I have to go," she said, doing her best to convey how sorry she was. "I'm so sorry. It's an emergency."

She was prepared for the sad expressions, but she wasn't prepared for the support she saw in Samuel's eyes. "It's okay," he said. "Is there anything I can do?"

Leah shook her head. "It's…I have to go," she managed, trying her best to hold back the emotions she thought she'd zipped up before she came into the room. She didn't fight him as he put his arms around her. Just put her head on his shoulder, let him comfort her, let herself be comforted for the last time.

And when she lifted her head as the phone buzzed in her pocket, she met the warmth in his eyes.

"Gotta go," she said. "I'll call you when this gets settled."

He didn't say anything, just squeezed her hand before letting it drop.

But two steps to the door, she stopped, turned around, and followed the path of his cheekbones with her fingers, and kissed him.

This time, when she left, she closed the door behind herself, got into the car and drove away.

Chapter Twenty-Two

IT WAS RAINING when Samuel got the call from Leah to meet him at the MMJH. But he walked to the subway station and rode into Manhattan. It was still raining when he got off the subway, raining on 16th street as he walked in.

Same exhibit profiling Abraham Kaplan of Abe's Kitchen greeted him just off the side of the entrance, a video tape playing on a loop.

But all that mattered was Leah.

She stood just in front of the entrance to the Abe Kaplan exhibit, her hair long, her rain boots peeking out from under her jeans, a cardigan sweater hugging her curves.

She was spectacular and yet it was as if she sucked all the light inside, locking it away.

All he wanted to do was hold her.

But she'd never let him. Not like this.

Instead, he smiled. "So we're getting our museum day?" he asked.

Her smile was sad, and all it made him want to do was put his arms around her. To comfort her in ways that she rarely let anybody. "Yeah."

It was an exhibit of art created by Jewish athletes, and he'd thought of her when he saw it. Immediately.

His brother had wondered why he'd been so interested in a random art exhibit like it, but to him this wasn't random. This was Leah.

"I couldn't wait to show you," he said. "I just am glad I'm getting the chance to."

He could see she wanted to smile but there was something stopping her. "Are you okay?"

She didn't answer, just took his hand. "Let's walk through the exhibit," she said. "We need to talk afterwards anyway."

Her tone was ominous, but he knew if he pushed, he wouldn't get anything out of her. So he nodded and walked through the halls of the museum, his fingers entwined with hers.

But they stopped at a glass exhibit case, and she pointed, the bright nail polish on her fingers leading the way, the lights on a runway. "It's why I left the party."

He looked closer, recognizing the item in the case as a mask, the mask he'd contributed lettering to at the Tzedakah Exchange gala. "You left because of a mask?"

She laughed, and for a second the sadness he saw in her dissipated. "No," she said once she'd regained her composure. "I left because of a client. The client that inspired the mask."

He nodded, but he didn't think she was going to give

him more, not there and not with that expression on her face.

"Anyway," she said as she dropped his hand. "There are always clients and stories and things, but the way ours goes now needs to be private. Do you want to come over to my place? I'm closer."

His jaw dropped and he didn't know what was happening. "Um…of course?"

"To talk," she said. "Although it's probably better if we go to the Stars and Icing I saw on the corner. Better place to chat."

Which meant a few things. She was managing reactions.

But all the same, it seemed like she was holding back.

What was going on?

He nodded. "Okay."

IT WAS A bright, beautiful, Manhattan afternoon when Leah left the museum, Samuel walking by her side. She'd shoved her hands into her pockets to keep from reaching out, the same way she'd reached out to him so many times before.

If this day was different, she'd be walking with him, their fingers intertwined like their lives had become. But now, they were tangled, twisted, knotted, on the way to being cut thread by thread.

Truth to tell, Leah realized the threads that connected

them had been cut long before. She'd been thinking the worst as she left Liam's party but the days of all-nighters, where Carly's contract and her next cup of coffee had been the only things on her mind followed one after the other. This contract had been harder to negotiate than any other she'd ever done, but it was important. The time was worth it, and when the negotiations had finished, Leah wanted to collapse and she had.

Until she remembered that the outside world called and Samuel left texts and emails.

Each text, each email fed into her guilt, draining her and reminding her why she was a horrible bet.

Now, she and Samuel had settled into one of the small booths in the back of the 13th Street location of Stars and Icing, the chocolate pudding freeze they'd ordered in beautiful glass bowls in front of them.

And yet all of the chocolate in the world couldn't support her through this conversation, and soothe the wound she was about to create. Sometimes, the things she had to do were painful, but there was no choice.

None.

"So," he said. "Are you okay?"

Which was one of those million-dollar questions; innocuous, and yet not at the same time. Pointed. "No," she said. "I'm not okay."

He nodded, and she could see his body change, from the slight relaxation of someone about to eat dessert to someone who was bracing themselves. "What's wrong?"

Now she was in it. Now she had to say something, and make it clear, whatever it is. "I can't do this," she managed. "I can't continue with the contract."

If she concentrated, she thought she might hear the sound of his jaw breaking on the table, but it only looked that wide. His eyes looked like endless chocolate pools of sadness, which hurt.

"What?"

"I know," she managed. "I thought…but I don't…won't have the time to do the emotional work that a real relationship—what you deserve—requires. My job is always going to intervene. My life isn't mine and that isn't fair."

"So that's it?"

She nodded, quickly, trying not to consider the way his words stung. "Yes," she said. "I can't continue on like this, knowing I'm going to hurt you for real. I can't do that."

"So you're going to leave at the first sign of trouble? Not even give me a chance to work things out with you?"

She shook her head. "You saw what happened when I let my guard down and relaxed. My job intervened and I couldn't get back to you, or anybody, for a week at least. I just… I can't."

"I can work anywhere," he said. "I can get lost in work for hours. I can sit and do my work in the stands of a hockey game…"

"It doesn't matter because my job isn't just sitting there.

It's focusing on what's going on. I can't be without a phone ever, and I can't give you what you deserve," she managed even as her heart was breaking. "I can't. I just can't. But I can give you something else?"

He blinked; he was confused. She understood that much.

"I forgive you," she said. "For high school. You've matured, you've changed. We're different people now, and it's not fair to let you believe that I still harbor that kind of upset."

He looked like he'd gotten hit by a truck and all she wanted to do was break down and tell him that she could stay with him, that she could be with him. But the thought of cold hard reality was making her nauseous.

"Thank you," he said, finally. "I appreciate that."

She could see he was having trouble figuring out what to do and how to handle things. This conversation, their connection, heck. Anything and everything.

But he sat there, across from her, his hands just behind the border of being able to touch her. And then he clenched his fingers and let them go. She followed his movements, wanting to take that step of touching his fingers with hers.

She couldn't take refuge in his touch any longer, nor could she ease the pain he was visibly feeling. She was having enough trouble as it was keeping her own swirling storm of emotion locked away inside. "Is there anything else I can do? Do you need help?"

He shook his head, then paused, as if he'd remembered

the section of the contact where he'd asked for consideration, for a favor to be granted later.

And if nothing else, now could be that later.

"I've got a big contract coming," he said. "But I need an agent. If you know anybody, can you send them my way?"

"I can do that," she said, pushing the words out as quickly as she could. "I know someone who might be helpful."

"I'd appreciate that," he said. "So I guess this it?"

She nodded. "This is it." And then she stood up. "I have to go," she said before she lost it completely in front of him.

Second thoughts, third thoughts followed her out of the restaurant and onto the subway that took her back to her apartment.

She was alone, and that was how it was meant to be.

Right?

Chapter Twenty-Three

SAMUEL MANAGED TO get on the subway, leaving the chocolate pudding and his drink behind.

The darkness of the tunnel that connected Manhattan and Queens suited his mood as it was. He'd gotten forgiveness from Leah, the one thing he'd always wanted, the one thing he'd always hoped for.

And yet, why did it feel like he'd been given the worst sort of consolation prize?

Why did it feel like he'd lost?

Because he had. He'd lost Leah.

And so when he got into his apartment, he locked the door, ignored his phone, grabbed some popcorn and watched the Shadow Squad movies on his favorite streaming service in an attempt to clear his head and remind himself of the other things going on in his life.

What felt like millions and zero hours later, after the last movie was done, he headed off to bed.

The next morning, he braced himself before checking his phone.

Nothing from Leah, which was to be expected.

It still hurt.

But he had gotten a text from Oliver, asking if he wanted to catch up and grab coffee with him, and if he hadn't had to ask Oliver professional questions, he would have stayed home.

Which was a far cry from an answer he would have given six months ago, and yet there he was.

But what kind of person would he be if he left people hanging?

What kind of professional would he be if he let huge opportunities go by the wayside?

What kind of partner for Leah could he be if he dropped everything and hid at the first sign of weakness? Because that's something she never did. Leah was tenacious and smart. She was a woman in a profession still dominated by men, with clients prepared to do great things.

Because no matter what happened between them, in order to deal with his own issues, he needed to become, if not remain, someone who'd make Leah believe it was possible to have a good, strong, clear relationship.

Someone who used his time effectively, someone who understood the time she needed.

Which meant he had to find himself an agent who could make clear the mess of the contract Liam was going to send him.

He'd asked Leah for recommendations, but he could ask

Oliver.

Oliver had worked with Liam before, which meant there was a good chance the man had an agent. And so he got off the subway near the café Oliver wanted to meet at, full of purpose, eyes wide and bushy-tailed.

"Glad you came," Oliver said.

"Thanks for asking me," he said. "How are you doing?"

"Good. How are you?"

And *that* was the question, wasn't it. Samuel didn't feel up to diving into the whole story, updating Oliver about what had happened since the party, at least not yet. So he chose to avoid the subject.

"Trying to focus on other things," he said with a laugh."

"Things aren't good with Leah?"

What was it with people and how observant they are? "Long story," he said, in a second effort to change the subject while at the same time giving him…something. "But I'm trying to be the person who would be good for her, no matter what's going on with us."

"Which is actually a smart way to handle it. Coming from, you know…" Oliver said.

He laughed. "Someone in a very long-term committed relationship?"

Oliver nodded. "Got it in one. So aside from the fact you're fixing things, what's going on?"

What better time than the present to dive into the specifics of the situation. "I need an agent," he said. "If the thing is going to happen that we can't talk about, then I'm going to need an agent to go through that contract."

"When it happens," Oliver qualified. "Because you know it's coming. And my agent's name is Ryan Kaplan."

He put the name in his notes app.

"Ryan's closed to queries at the moment," Oliver continued, much to Samuel's utter surprise. "But he'll definitely look at people who are referred to him working on a project he's interested in."

"Thanks," he said. "I appreciate that."

"Good," Oliver said with a smile. "Now. What else are you going to do to get your house in order?"

He was going to answer until his phone buzzed with an incoming email.

The email was an introduction email from Leah.

And Ryan Kaplan.

From: LNachman@allsportsagency.com
To: rkaplan@HalloranKaplanlit.com,
slevine@levinesofer.com

Sending a connection email to brilliant letterer Samuel Levine, who I've known since childhood, who's in need of an agent, and agent Ryan Kaplan, a friend of mine from law school.

Which would have been great on its own, but there was also a reply from Ryan Kaplan.

From: RKaplan@HalloranKaplanLit.com
To: LNachman@allsportsagency.com,
slevine@levinesofer.com

Leah: Thanks for the intro

Samuel: I'd love to talk about your portfolio and your upcoming projects. My slate is pretty full, but with a recommendation from Leah, as well as a reminder that you worked on the posters I loved for a media project based on another client's books, you certainly fit the referral, as well as the samples required for someone who letters in the way you do.

If you can speak to one of my clients and have them send a note, that would be great but not mandatory. Otherwise, please contact me at your earliest convenience to discuss representation.

Ryan

Was he reading this correctly?

Was he…

Did it just…

"Samuel? What's going on? Are you okay?"

He pulled himself away from the screen and nodded. "Sorry," he said. "I think your agent wants to represent me. Leah sent him an email and might want a client reference."

"You kidding me?" Oliver grinned. "Of course I'll send that email. Right now. We worked on that logo together, after all. Not to mention we're working on that project together. And don't say it's not happening, because it is."

Just like that, the item he focused on getting checked off his list was on its way to being in his inbox. And no matter what Liam did with the contract, or didn't, he would have an agent who would deal with the comics side of his career that would take stress off of Tommy. And, of course Aaron.

Now it was time to enjoy his coffee with Oliver. Things were looking up, even though he had to focus on his accomplishments one by one.

And picture Leah smiling at him as he completed each task.

LEAH WAS EXHAUSTED. Exhausted but accomplished and, as she walked into the office on Monday afternoon, she received emails from both Ryan and Samuel, thanking her for connecting them.

It took a great deal to not send a gushing email to Samuel, but she didn't.

Instead, she closed her office door and checked her email, starting to prep for the rest of the day.

One foot in front of the other.

Until there was a knock at her door.

"Come in," she said.

"Leah." Bruck walked into the office, a smile on his face. "Congratulations."

"Thanks," she said, smiling. She was used to putting on

masks, hiding her emotions. This was no different. The very last thing she wanted to do was smile; she was tired, proud of the work she'd done. But she still felt like there was a hole in her heart.

"Did you get everything you wanted from the Empires?"

And that was the question, wasn't it.

"I got a lot of it," she said. "The most important things. Guarantee of MHL playing time, the crisis PR person on staff. A few of their players worked with someone a few years ago, so they're going to see if he's interested."

Bruck shook his head. "MHL playing time?"

Leah nodded. "We're not doing this for a stunt," she said. "If she's going to sign, if we're going to do this, she's going to do this. If she's going to be buried in the minors, she could play with the Legends. The minors isn't worth the nonsense she could be put through. Name on the back of her jersey is only going to save her so much."

"Independent analysis, I'm thinking?"

Leah nodded. "Because I'm not dealing with someone who theoretically believes a woman can play, until she's standing right in front of him, potentially pitching a shutout only to have the team lose the game because she got stuck on the bench for the third."

"Hardball," he said. "I like it."

Which was good, considering how easy it was for her to lose herself in work, in her job. "Thank you," she said. "I thought it was risky, but I figured this kind of situation was important enough."

"If you're negotiating with a team for an unprecedented contract, it's expected that agents at our level, who have our kind of experience and our sort of leverage, are going to play hardball."

She bit her lip. "Our?"

He nodded, and her heart stopped. "I've looked over the numbers, watched you perform and decided it's officially time to ask you to join as a partner. And maybe possibly, see what you might think about taking over on the day I'm ready to walk out that door."

And if her heart had stopped before, it had completely flatlined now.

Not just partner, but…successor?

"You're…asking me to succeed you and take over the agency when you're ready to retire?"

"Yes," he said with a smile. "Will you want to take the step, be a partner in the agency for the next three to six years and then take over?"

"If you give me a notarized statement to that effect," she said with a laugh, "that'll be the best offer I've ever had. Thank you."

"Yep. I've made the right decision," Bruck said with a smile. "You've learned a great deal. Now we're going to do more. I'm going to train you for real. You ready?"

Leah nodded. "I am. Thank you."

"Good." Bruck smiled. "Good that you have a good

partner around at home. Having a partner who gets our job and what we do is important for your mental health."

She nodded. She knew that. But she wasn't going to tell Bruck that the relationship between her and Samuel was over. Not at all.

"My wife," he continued, "I told you that she was impressed with your young man, hm? Talented guy. Devoted to you."

Samuel was all of those things, but all she could do was nod. "He liked talking to her," she managed.

As the conversation continued, more and more, Leah wished she could tell Samuel. Talk to him, celebrate her success with him.

Truly share her life with him.

But how?

How could she do this?

All she knew was that she needed to convince him and herself that not only did she need him back into her life, but also that she had the emotional and mental space to not only get him back, but also to keep him.

She didn't know where to start, but she was playing for keeps this time.

Chapter Twenty-Four

As he tried to figure out what his next steps were, which of his commissions and assignments had to be prioritized, Samuel's phone buzzed.

It was Bryce Emerson.

He picked up the phone. "Hello?"

"Hey, listen. I need a favor."

"Okay?"

"A friend of mine convinced me to teach the 14U boys' hockey team based at the Briarwood JCC about masks, and how I use writing techniques in making them. Apparently they're having trouble with all of that?"

Samuel nodded. A boys' hockey team based at the Briarwood JCC wanting a guest speaker to talk about writing techniques.

There was only one writing technique a hockey team full of twelve-year-old boys would be having trouble with.

"I'm guessing the kind of trouble they're having is with script?"

"Yeah," Bryce said with a laugh. "Got it in one. From the way Ash tells it, these boys are stressing, even in the summer over this."

Wait.

Who was Bryce talking about? "Ash?"

"Mendel," Bryce clarified as if it wasn't important. "You know, Judith Nachman's fiancé? My wife's agent's future brother-in-law? That one."

Right. Leah's future brother-in-law, part of the couple he'd been contracted to make a ketubah for on the day this whole adventure with Leah started again.

Threads. Tied. Pulling him and Leah together. Again.

Yes, it didn't matter so much that they had untied for now; if nothing else, this invitation would be a sign that he could fix this.

That he and Leah could tie themselves together again.

But Bryce didn't need to hear this, not yet, if at all. "Okay," he said, because Bryce did in fact need an answer, even though he hadn't actually asked a question. "So what's the favor?"

"So considering the location and the team," Bryce began, "I thought of the mask we did."

The mask. The one he worked on after the long session at Bryce's house, the one where Leah drove him to the mechanic's to pick up his car.

But once again, Bryce didn't need to hear that. Instead he said, "Yeah. I had a great time. It's a great collaboration, was, actually."

Bryce continued, "If you're up for it, you could join me

and talk about the way you used the writing techniques both with the mask, and the way you letter the ketubahs and mezuzahs, as well as comics."

Which put everything together. What Bryce really wanted was for him to talk about the way he used Hebrew calligraphy as well as script. And that sounded fun. "I like the sound of that," he said. "What day?"

"Thursday."

Perfect. He had time to prep, get back to Briarwood and do the class. He nodded. "At the Briarwood JCC? Do you want to meet somewhere to go over things before heading over there?"

"Yep. I'll text you more details when I have them, and that sounds like a good idea."

Not just good. But great. Because that meant he'd get a chance to talk to someone who might understand the best way to get through to Leah.

AS MONDAY TURNED into Tuesday, Leah had put together and discarded so many different solutions to the problem she'd created with Samuel, she was going to lose her mind.

It felt as if the more she tried to figure out a solution, the further away one was.

Which meant desperate measures were called for. She needed help.

Naomi and Livvy had been lovely, but the last serious conversation she'd had with Naomi about the specifics of her situation with Samuel involved a rather large reminder that both of them were single. Not that single people couldn't help her fix her romantic problems, the feeling she'd gotten was that neither of them felt comfortable.

Not that she was upset with them about it; it just made her feel alone, which was the complete opposite of the fellowship of the cousins group her sister had pulled together all those years ago.

Except that left two people. And there was no way she'd ask Judith. The very last thing she wanted was a conversation with her sister about how the situation with Samuel had progressed since the wedding expo, not to mention she didn't need either Judith's judgment nor her attempt to fix the situation.

This was her own situation to fix, after all. Not her sister's.

Which left one final option.

Shayna, of all people, had been the least judgmental and the most helpful of all her close female relatives. She'd made space and created time.

Which meant during an hour she'd pulled together in the middle of a ridiculously busy workday, she relented and called her sister-in-law.

"What's up?"

She briefly explained the situation to her sister-in-law. "I don't know what to do," she admitted. "I don't know how to fix this…situation with Samuel."

"Okay. I'm getting that you don't do this often, so first of all, I'm thrilled you're coming to me."

"Well," Leah said, "you've been the most understanding and supportive through this whole situation. Of course I'm talking to you."

"Thank you," Shayna replied after a moment. "I appreciate it, you know, the vote of confidence or confidante if that's a phrase."

Leah smiled even though she knew Shayna couldn't see her. "Whatever it is, it works. But yeah."

"So," Shayna continued, "what I do know, speaking of working, is that man cares for you. Don't forget, I watched him when we were waiting for the valet at the gala. He was so lovely to Ramona, so sweet generally. And not that he's not the sort of guy who would have done it otherwise, but I think a lot of that has to do with the fact that he cares for you."

There was a silence that followed, as if Shayna wanted to make sure what she'd said had sunk in. "Not only that, you have to realize that the man knows you, or should. You didn't, hopefully, say something too awful to him, right?"

Leah paused. "No…"

"You didn't threaten him with bodily harm, right?"

"No."

Though Leah had no idea where her sister-in-law was

headed at this point.

"Which means," Shayna said, "is there an event still there in the contract, and yes I know you said you wanted to end it, but maybe?"

"I could," she managed, "ask him if he wanted to go to Shabbas? Still?"

"You could," Shayna replied. "Have him come to ours for Shabbas and maybe, you know, tell him how you feel there?"

Which was of course the idea that made the most sense. "That works," she said.

But sense didn't mean reality. Sense didn't have anything to do with her and Samuel, not really. Not when they were kids and not now, especially when, well it wasn't him convinced they were...

Bashert.

All she'd been was convinced they were made up of messy, tangled threads.

What if she'd come to the realization that the threads weren't tangled but tied together too late? What if her realization that nothing she did, no time she spent, was worth a damn if she didn't have him to share it with, came after he'd decided she was right?

What if he'd decided that she wasn't worth it?

"I mean..." she said, because if she was going to confide in Shayna, she might as well go for the gold. "Would he listen to me? Would he accept my invitation? Would I be too late? Am I too late?"

"You can't say for sure," Shayna said. "And nobody can ever say anything definitively for sure."

Which was helpful.

Not.

"But," Shayna continued after Leah realized she hadn't said anything. "I would bet on the fact that someone who's wanted someone and something for so long isn't going to give up on it easily. Nobody ever does. He may drive a hard bargain."

"Like what hard bargain?" Because if she knew nothing else, it was how to negotiate and bargain. She'd been doing so for most of her professional life.

"Probably not kneel like some books I've read, but like probably make you actually admit you were wrong. Or something."

"So like some visible grovel?" she wondered, just to make sure.

"Audible grovel," Shayna said. "Some clear indication. But you'll be fine. I think."

She hoped. Except how she'd be able to bargain with him on a grovel was beyond her; this wasn't Passover and the search for the afikomen when she was a kid, but something else.

This would, as they said, be the bargain of her life.

How she'd manage that, she had no idea. But that at least gave her a goal.

But Shayna was still on the other end and she'd done a big favor, even if it didn't feel so big. "Thank you," she finally said. "How can I repay you?"

"First," Shayna said. "Thursday night you need to come and visit; I've got a thing to go to. It's a jewelry designer's thing for the Unicorns."

Which meant her sister-in-law needed a partner in crime for a girls' night out. "Okay."

"Designer's a Jamie Sawyer…"

The name sounded familiar and Leah let it play over and over in her mind.

Sawyer. Jamie…jewelry designer…Sawyer.

And then she had it.

The conversation at Liam's party, where she stood and laughed with Sarah. "She was at the party I went to with Samuel."

Jamie would know how to fix this; if nothing else, she was friendly with the group.

"That's good," Shayna said. "Even better idea to come to the showing."

And as she ended the call with her sister-in-law, Leah felt excited and energized for the first time in days. She was going to figure this whole mess out.

Somehow.

Chapter Twenty-Five

BRYCE EMERSON WAS easy to work with; Samuel knew that pretty well. Not only as an artistic collaborator, but now as a speaker.

As they headed into the JCC, Bryce turned toward him. "You ready for this?"

Samuel nodded. "Yep. Just like we discussed. Which I'm glad we did."

"It was a good idea," Bryce said. "Good to outline..." And then he paused, making Samuel wonder what was going on. "Asher, Good to see you."

Samuel turned to meet Judith Nachman's fiancé for the first time; he knew about the man from the information and the photos he was using to make the ketubah but had never actually seen him in person.

"Good to see you too, Bryce, Thanks for coming."

"Not a problem. And I've got a collaborator."

Asher Mendel's eyes turned onto him. "I see that." He paused. "We'll talk later, after class because I think you've got some planning to do."

He wasn't sure what Asher was talking about, but he

nodded all the same.

"Good. Nephew's here, and we're ready to go. Come on in," Asher continued, ushering them into the room.

The beginnings, the attendance and other organizational things went quickly and then it was their turn. Of course, nothing ever went perfectly, but Samuel was enjoying every second of this class.

Arguably, his favorite part was hearing the kids say phrases like "That was fascinating," or "I've never thought of it that way before," as he spoke about certain aspects of his career that reminded him of the things these kids must go through when they were on the ice. This kind of conversation, and this kind of direct impact, wasn't usually part of his job description, at least not for longer than the five minutes he met people at expos or cons, but it was…nice.

Seeing their eyes widen when his points were expanded by listening to Bryce Emerson talk about what he did was simply icing on the cake.

"What are your future plans?" Bryce asked him as a way of continuing the conversation.

And of course, there were a bunch of kids who raised their hands.

"Are you going to do more posters?" one of the kids wondered.

"Are you going to make a Torah?" asked another.

He laughed, both lucky and thrilled that his future career choices mattered to these kids in some way. "Well," he said.

"Definitely some more posters, because I love working with the teams responsible for them. And I'm not going to do a Torah just yet, but later on down the line for sure."

And that was that, the end of the class.

"Great job," Bryce said as the kids left the room.

"Thanks for coming," Asher added. "They really enjoyed themselves."

"So did I," Samuel replied. "Glad I came."

"And," Asher said with a laugh, "this is how we do things. This is how we bring people together, and try to make him realize what kind of gold he has in my future sister-in-law."

It took him a second to realize what Asher had said. "Uh…"

"Family gossip," Asher said with a grin. "My fiancée is invested."

"So that's why you were at the practice a few weeks ago," Bryce said as if he was putting it all together.

"Not really," he said. "It's how I learned about the practice and why Leah drove me to the mechanics after the art session."

"So," Asher said. "What's up with you and Leah?"

And now the question he wasn't expecting, but figured he'd end up answering anyway. "We're figuring things out."

Which was a general statement, and could be interpreted a billion different ways. Hopefully the look exchanged between Bryce and Asher wasn't exactly the strange thing he thought it was.

"What's there to figure out?"

Of course. "I mean..."

"You need to figure out how you're going to get to Shabbat dessert on Friday."

"Shim...really?"

The kid, Shim, had to be Leah's nephew, little Ramona's big brother. "Said goodbye to everybody so I'm ready, Uncle Ash," the kid continued. "And why is this a surprise?"

"What do you mean?" Bryce said, because Samuel couldn't figure out how to answer this.

"I mean," Shim continued, "figuring it out means they're fighting so he has to fix it. With babka."

Asher and Bryce both laughed, making him feel really awful. "Very astute," Asher said. "He right?"

Having decided that everything was going to be on the table as it was, he nodded. "We're not fighting," he said. "But I want to make it clearer where I stand so that she feels more secure."

"Babka," Shim said. "That's the ticket."

"How long have you known each other?" Asher said. "I mean my fiancée tells me you went to high school together? That you're a Briarwood guy?"

"Born and raised," he admitted. "Your fiancée is older by a few years, but Leah and I made our way through the Briarwood schools together."

"So," Asher continued, "what is the story between you

and Leah? What's been…the issue?"

And so, deciding that he needed to talk this through, he told Asher and Bryce most of the story, at least as much as he felt comfortable saying in front of Shim.

"So," Bryce said. "Seems pretty obvious to me."

"This I have to hear," Asher said with a laugh.

But Samuel wasn't laughing. He'd been trying to figure out what the best way was to convince Leah that he wasn't going anywhere, wasn't going to push, and wasn't going to leave in a huff.

Unless that was what Leah told him she wanted.

And if Bryce had a suggestion, then he'd take it.

"Ash and Shim want you to come to Shabbat dinner on Friday. Go. Bring something symbolic. If it's babka, it's babka. If it's something else, bring something else. Whatever it is," Bryce said, "make it clear that you've been listening. Not just to her words, but the things she isn't saying, or hasn't been saying."

"But," Asher said. "Bring babka so that Shayna'll let you in the house."

And now he had a plan, but more importantly, he had allies.

THE COMMUNITY ROOM of the Briarwood JCC was decorated with twinkling lights, and Leah had no idea what to make of it.

"This is..."

"They have a thing," Shayna said. "They're not as...much as the Westchester ice unicorn herd, but it's a thing."

A thing it was, Leah thought, but managed not to say under her breath. Rainbow ombré reflected off the bar, attendees were in various states of glitter and jewels.

Was this a party or an exhibition?

And yet in that instant, Leah understood why Shayna'd asked her to come.

Naomi would be critiquing, Liv would be drowning, and Judith? Lord knew what her sister would do. She was Shayna's safe choice, adaptable but not distracting. Helpful but not overwhelming. And on a night where she was attending as a mom, Shayna needed help.

"Okay," Leah said, now confident in her role. "Let's do this."

Shayna smiled as they began to head through the maze of tables.

But the only thing Leah could think of as they walked through, seeing the range of items was: "This is one artist?"

Shayna nodded. "Supposedly. I know, right?"

"Like how much of a collection would one artist have to have if the exhibition space would be this big?"

"Let's just say," said a familiar voice, "that the last party I threw didn't have Pictionary, and not for another reason."

Jamie. "Hiii," Leah said. "This is gorgeous."

Jamie beamed. "Thank you. Didn't expect to see you here, but I am very glad to see a familiar face."

"I have to say that when my sister-in-law," Leah said gesturing at Shayna, "suggested I come tonight; the fact that it was your collection was an incentive."

"Yep." Shayna grinned. "My daughter's on the team, so Leah's here as a proud auntie."

"Oh that's great." Jamie looked between them, and Leah figured that there was going to be an invitation issued, probably to talk about Samuel.

"Are you going to have time to catch up in a bit? I want to know what's going on with Samuel."

Just as predicted, Leah thought to herself. But all the same, Shayna snorted. "Don't we all."

"I may need some help," Leah said.

Jamie raised an eyebrow. "Oh really."

And then she paused, making Leah wonder if something else was going on.

"Looking for something in particular in the meanwhile?"

Leah sighed. "I want to give someone something that will make this person understand that I don't make decisions lightly, that I've always...had feelings, that I'm not going to change."

She looked in between Jamie and Shayna only to realize from their surprised and thoughtful expressions that she'd either said too much, made the wrong decision or both. "Um," she managed. "Never mind. It's fine..."

"So," Jamie said, breaking the silence and most likely going to barge past the tape she'd put on the door she'd opened. "You can always buy something new—I've got a few interesting pen-themed things, for example, but the biggest thing you can do is show him, whoever he may be, that you have been paying attention. Something older that might symbolize the fact that despite everything, all the water under the bridge between the both of you, your feelings have never changed."

And as they walked through the showing, Leah realized there was something. She bought a pair of pen cufflinks and a pen tie tack, knowing all too well that the item she needed most was at her apartment, and she'd need help bringing it back to Briarwood.

Chapter Twenty-Six

IT WAS A gorgeous Friday afternoon. The sun was shining, and Aaron's car was speeding up the highway, precious cargo in the trunk. The babka was on Samuel's lap and life was good.

So was the conversation. Tommy was talking about something happening with one of the baseball teams he followed, and Aaron was asking about a documentary that Tommy had watched.

Very familiar, very comfortable.

Except there was something that Samuel needed to do. If he had a chance of making it out the door in time to catch dessert at the Nachmans', Samuel had to inform his brother about what was going on, and maybe enlist his help in getting out the door.

Which wouldn't be possible if either his brother or his brother-in-law stood in his way.

"So," Samuel said as Aaron drove up the highway toward Briarwood, "I'm going to leave before dinner's over, take care of some business at the Nachmans'."

There was silence in the car, and Samuel could see his

brother do his best to glare in the rearview mirror. "You're doing what?"

"Watch the road," Tommy interjected, thankfully. "Stop glaring at your brother."

Yep. As far as Samuel was concerned, there were, in fact, benefits to delivering this information in the car where Aaron was driving and Tommy was sitting in the passenger seat.

And yet he still had the question to answer. Or rather the information to deliver once again. "I'm going to Nathan and Shayna Nachman's place tonight after dinner, hopefully to catch dessert."

There was a long pause before Aaron answered. "I'm not sure whether I'm more offended by you leaving us with Mom and Dad or you taking the babka."

"The babka," said Tommy, sure of himself and his husband, and of course most likely correct. "Because you don't know what's going on and whether you think they deserve the babka."

"Right you are," Aaron replied as Samuel added an internal tick mark to the score he was keeping. "Okay then. So?"

Now was the fun part. Samuel managed to find the words to explain what had been going on with Leah, at least the best way he could. "So anyway," he said, "when both Leah's nephew and future brother-in-law told me that I needed to come tonight, I realized I needed to make it count."

"So you're going to hope that the babka is enough to convince Leah that you're worthy of the time she has?"

He shook his head. Aaron and his obsession with babka that was or was not his amused him. "Babka is for her family," Samuel clarified for his brother's benefit and need to know where all babka was at all times. "The reason I asked you to drive with your larger car is what I'm hoping to use to convince Leah I'm worthy."

"Speaking of using things," Aaron said. "I liked your letter to the congregation in Virginia."

Going from babka to work matters, but that was also normal—if not slightly dizzying—conversation between him and Aaron. All the same, Samuel adjusted himself to the swerve in topic and nodded. "I think I'd like to prepare myself to write a Sefer Torah in the future, but I'm not ready, not now."

"Indulge me," interjected Tommy. "But what exactly do you have in that back seat? Do we need to worry about the condition of the trunk after you take it out?"

From the back, Samuel laughed. This wasn't Tommy's car exactly, but it was enough his for him to be interested in the condition of the car. But the idea, the contents?

What sat in the trunk, the object of Tommy's concern, had been the result of a random idea…and yet it seemed like it would possibly, potentially work. He'd listened to Bryce and Asher and Shim and, in the end, Samuel decided that what was really important was a fresh start. And the item he brought needed to symbolize that, not a recycled piece of someone else's history, or even their own.

So when he'd gotten back to his apartment after the class on Thursday, he'd racked his brain, trying to figure out something that would be symbolic enough to fit the situation. To demonstrate that his mind wasn't on the past, that it was on the possibilities of their history, their future.

Something new.

And then it clicked.

He'd stood, staring at it as if he'd seen it for the first time. Leah had even pointed it out so long ago while they were talking about contracts.

This was it.

And so he managed to wrap it up, frame and all, and hope his brother, with the bigger car and the bigger trunk space, would be able to bring him to Briarwood.

"No," he said. "It's not a messy thing, just big."

Tommy snorted. "Hopefully it's big enough to do what you need it to."

And as Aaron turned into their parents' driveway, Samuel nodded. "Yep. That's what I'm hoping too."

LEAH KNEW EXACTLY what she had to do the second Jamie's words had sunk in. They followed her back to Manhattan right after the jewelry opening, followed her to bed and into her dreams that night.

Friday morning, standing in front of her closet, knowing the large wrapped package was inside, she made the executive decision to call Naomi. "I need you," she said. "It's an emergency."

"Okay?" Naomi sounded confused, but that was okay.

"I need you to help me bring a painting to Shayna's."

"A painting?

"A print, something, whatever it is," she said, knowing that all she'd been doing was carting it around the country with her, not opening it. She hadn't actually looked at it, didn't even know what condition it was in since she'd wrapped it up the first time one week before the infamous high school breakup.

Which was a problem.

"Right," Naomi said, interrupting Leah's train of thought. "I need to meet Livvy in Briarwood before Shabbas so it's a good choice."

"Good. I'm glad. Meet me at my place as soon as you can."

Of course a few hours later, she was settled with her cousin in the car on the way to Briarwood, the painting strapped in the back. "Thank you," she managed. "I appreciate this."

Naomi said, "I have one question."

"Okay?"

"What's this for?"

Which wasn't the question Leah expected her cousin to ask, but she went with it anyway. "It's a very long overdue gift to someone who I've always been tied to."

"Tied to?" Naomi said. "Um…"

"Did you ever know that strings and being tied together are cross-cultural when talking about relationships and people?" Leah asked instead of admitting it. "Tangled webs that tie people together, red string of fate, the strings that tie you to your bashert, invisible strings that connect people? They're all slight variations on the same idea, and I think it's very cool."

"You're seriously talking about philosophy right now?" Naomi asked. "That could only mean one thing."

"What?"

"Samuel. You're really feeling things about Samuel."

Instead of denying it, she nodded. "And hopefully this painting will also be what reminds him that I don't just have them now. That no matter what's happened between us, no matter how much I've tried to deny it, I always have felt things about Samuel."

"Who are you and what happened to my cousin?"

Leah laughed. "Yeah. I don't know. Life? Miracles? Fate…"

"If you say some variation of fate one more time…" Naomi quipped. "Now, to avoid the fate conversation, I have another question for you."

"What?"

"Why am I here and not Judith?"

There were so many reasons, but Leah focused on the important ones, the positives. "You and Shayna have been there for me through this whole adventure. You didn't judge me, didn't stare and hope for more when I told you what I thought was going on. So I called you."

Naomi nodded. "Thank you," she said.

"You're welcome." And as they turned in to Shayna's house, Leah realized that she was looking forward to whatever was coming next.

And she hoped she knew what it was.

CHALLAH, CANDLES, WINE, dinner, not in that order, but those things combined with a white tablecloth and good people around the table made for the perfect Shabbas.

Tommy had his tsimmes, Aaron had to be stopped from taking most of the kugel, and there was soup, and his father's favorite matzah balls, that started everything off. There was even gefilte fish that reminded him of the conversation he'd had with Leah on a Queens night.

But after all of those appetizers and some amazing chicken, Samuel needed to go. "I love you all, but I need to head out for a brief second. You won't miss me," he said.

"You need the car keys?" Aaron asked under his breath.

Samuel appreciated that his brother was trying to be subtle, but this wasn't subtle on a Friday night, not to mention that Samuel had stashed the package upstairs in preparation for the need for a quick departure. "No," he said. "It's fine."

Aaron nodded, but the expression on his brother's face when he turned back toward Samuel looked like he'd been caught eternally silently screaming, jaw seconds from hitting the table. Because of course, it was Friday night and their father had a *look* on his face. Not just any look, but the indescribable look of incredulity, reserved only for the impossible.

His mother was the one who spoke; maybe she could be reasoned with—respect was necessary on a Friday night, no matter how old you were. Not only to family, but also the tradition.

"Where are you going?"

Samuel could almost hear his brother whispering to Tommy, probably something like 'this is going to be interesting' in not so dulcet tones. And yet at the same time, Samuel was very well aware that things would have been vastly different, and louder, had he not informed his brother and brother-in-law what was going to happen.

"To the Nachmans'," Samuel said. "I need to talk to Leah."

Predictably, his father, unimpressed, raised an eyebrow. "Before we're done you have to leave?"

And that was the crux of it all, wasn't it? Nobody left Shabbas dinner so quickly. But things were going to be different, and miracle of miracles, his mother smiled. "What, and not watch you sleep in front of the baseball game?"

"It's appointment viewing," his father replied, focused as usual on the years of tradition Samuel was about to break. "I can't sleep without his dulcet tones yelling about how annoying the announcers are."

Which they often were, unless the game was being broadcast on the home network. But that was another conversation for another time.

"Games on Union Sports," Tommy interjected. "So the announcers are fine."

"Let him go," Aaron added. "He's got to get his girl."

"You'll bring her back?"

Which was a question from his mother but could have been anybody asking.

"I might. But if there's news to tell, I'll tell you."

"Good," his mother said as his father and Tommy went off to watch the game. "I always liked her, and I never understood what happened. I hope the two of you can figure this out."

"Me too," he said, as he left the dining room and headed upstairs to grab the package, looking briefly in the mirror to make sure he didn't look awful.

Fixing that took some time, but when he was ready, he was clear that presentable was fine.

At least he thought so. All he knew, as he managed to get himself down the stairs and out the door into a beautiful

Briarwood summer night, was that he couldn't make a mistake. Not one.

Thankfully the location of Leah's family's Shabbas dinner wasn't that far, which meant a nice walk toward a very uncertain future. And he'd do this, he'd convince her. Step by step.

EVERYTHING HAD TO be perfect.

She barely managed to choke down dinner, Shayna's attempt at creating her version of a beef stew she'd been eyeing for years.

It might have a place in Jewish culinary history, but this version did not deserve a place on Shayna's regular menu. It was, to put it mildly, horrible.

"I don't understand," Shayna said. "I followed the instructions, used the perfect cuts of meat…and yet."

Thankfully, as everybody was discussing how to pronounce the name of this dish, Leah got up and left the room, grabbing the bag she'd left just outside Shayna's study.

Wine. Glasses. And the painting, perfectly propped up against a bookcase, still wrapped.

She stepped back and looked at her handiwork.

Perfect.

It had to be.

Of course, there wasn't even a knock, but the slight

creaking of door hinges.

"What..."

"So," Judith said, looking around. "What's going on?"

"This is private," Leah said. "Can you..."

"Go back to the rest of the family?" Judith shook her head.

Getting her sister out was going to be impossible.

"In fact," Judith continued as she barged her way into the room, "I'm wondering why you're creating what looks like a presentation area or, specifically an art gallery in Shayna's office?"

Answering the question without creating havoc meant giving more information than she actually wanted to. But Leah knew that she'd never hear the end of it if tonight happened, when Samuel showed up, if she didn't brief her sister in advance.

Which meant Leah had to start her tale at the beginning. "What you may or may not know is that after the expo, Samuel and I fake-dated. Contract, the whole deal."

Judith laughed, a deep belly laugh, with sparking eyes Leah hadn't seen from her sister in years. Which should have annoyed her, but for some reason it made Leah relax a bit more. "Are you kidding? Are you living HeartPix movies now?"

"HeartPix movies have people who didn't know each other fake-date," Leah explained, not arguing with her sister about why it felt so important to mention HeartPix movies.

"Same with dramas. And in both cases, the couple ends up as fake-dating fails because all these people know is the good side of the person they're contracted to…or otherwise fake dating. Samuel and I figured we'd stay fake and end with the contract because of our past. Anyway, don't mean to go into detail, but suffice to say, we dove in, partially because you've been on this 'everybody needs love' thing, and also the gossip after the expo."

"So it's my fault you're in the middle of a real-life yid-drama?"

Leah laughed despite the situation. "I figured that when Samuel and I broke up for good, you'd be happily married and your attention would be elsewhere, and not on me."

"There is a lot to unpack there," Judith said, "but you need to understand that I'm not going to stop worrying about you just because I'm married, or getting married. You're my baby sister, and you matter. Your life matters to me."

"Which I appreciate," Leah said with a grin. "As long as you worry about me less than your wedding or your marriage, I'm fine."

"Good. Glad to hear you appreciate my concern." But then Judith sat up in her chair and folded her arms as if she was getting ready to hear some kind of admission or confession. "But now what's this about the fact you're now also a fake-dating fail?"

"Yes," Leah managed. And so once again, she had to find

words that would explain the situation she and Samuel had been through, up until the point. "I think that like so many of the couples in the dramas, especially the MCs with busy lives, it's hard to see that it's not the quantity of free time but the quality of it, and who they spend that free time with. So basically, I need to explain to Samuel that I've always cared about him and that the feelings I've caught for him aren't recent. They've always been there."

"Wait," Judith managed amidst laughter that came out of nowhere. "Hold on a second. What is this? What are you saying?"

"I don't want to say that Samuel's my bashert, but what I will say is that it makes sense that so many cultures talk about relationships and couples through metaphors of tangled webs and strings that connect people. The private showing in here, you know, which is supposed to be private..."

"Yes," Judith said. "I realize you need your privacy."

"Thank you," Leah said. "So are you leaving?"

"I will, but you need to tell me that you're going to be as clear with Samuel about how you're feeling as you're being with me."

That was easy. "Yes," she said. "I'm going to be honest and vulnerable and lay my cards on the table, which is why I need the private showing."

"I'm impressed," Judith said.

Leah didn't know exactly what to say, so she went with

the basics. "Thank you?"

"You can do this," Judith continued, making Leah feel…things she wasn't ready to quantify. "And also, I'm right behind you. Even if you might not believe it."

"I do," she said, the words coming easily from a place deep inside of her. "I really do."

"And after you fix things?"

Leah raised an eyebrow; this conversation had gone way too easily and way too well for that statement. "Yes?"

"You might want to thank your nephew and your brother-in-law. And you might want to get the door before they do."

And as she left the room, Leah realized she'd never been so angry and yet thrilled at her sister's meddling.

SAMUEL WALKED DOWN the street, made the turn. Her parents weren't living there now; they were in Florida most of the time, but he'd made this walk often.

Same street, the one with the dead end that curved when you weren't paying attention. Her parents had kept their house in the single-story ranch style, but her brother had added a second story to his own house. On the same street as his parents.

His mind was going, recycling childhood memories and moments where he'd taken this walk on this street. He needed to focus.

And when he arrived at Nathan's house, where Leah was, his heart started to slam against his chest, so hard he was afraid it was going to push through. But he stopped on a neighbor's grass to try and collect himself package in hand.

As he headed up the driveway, he wondered if she'd be happy to see him or whether she'd slam the door in his face. Both were possible options, but he wanted to hope that if her family members were involved—her nephew and her future brother-in-law had both encouraged him—then there wasn't going to be a slam.

Even if there was, he wouldn't leave, wouldn't walk away. She was too important to walk away from. Finally, he was standing in front of the doorframe, wood and glass separating him from Leah.

He rang the doorbell, took a few deep breaths and waited.

The squeak of the door opening made his heart pound again, but Nathan's clear and obvious smile made him feel better.

"Oh good," Leah's older brother said. "You're here. I'll get..."

"Not necessary," Asher said as he appeared as if out of nowhere. "She's on her way; I hear the footsteps I think. All we have to do is look like we're talking and she'll..."

"What the heck is going on?"

And there she was—resplendent and gorgeous.

"You're here," she said.

"I'm here," he began, the words he wanted to say tripping on his tongue, wanting to get out. "I…"

And that was when Leah shook her head, her hair flying back and forth.

"We'll let you take over," Asher said, making his presence known as if he'd turned invisible for a moment.

"I'll deal with you two later," Leah said as he watched Asher and Nathan leave, Nathan giving a weird-looking thumbs up as he left.

"Don't mind them," she said.

And now he was alone with Leah, in the alcove of her brother's house, for the first time since the museum.

IT WAS THE noise she heard first as she emerged from Shayna's study, voices: Nathans and Asher's and Samuel's. There were people separating them but none of them mattered in this context.

She somehow managed to convince Nathan to leave, though Asher's involvement in this and that tie back to Judith had something to do with it for sure. But there she was, standing in front of him, his eyes wary, quizzical.

Samuel had never been quizzical before.

And he was holding a package.

"Leah," he said, "I…"

"Don't say anything," she said, "let me talk. Because if you start talking I'll never be able to get this out. And I have no idea what my brother-in-law or nephew did to get you here and I don't want to blow this."

He was silent, which was good.

"Come with me."

She didn't want to reach out her hand because hands before conclusions would always make her a terrible deal. So she took it for granted that he was following her through her brother's house, tried to focus and not listen to his footsteps.

Except this wasn't working either.

So, like Orpheus, she held out her hand. "Not looking back," she said, "but I'm hoping for a better ending."

Once again he didn't respond, but she did feel his fingers wrap around hers, giving her this ridiculously false sense of security because she knew that at any second, all of it could fall apart and no amount of armor would fix that.

Finally, she arrived at Shayna's study and she walked in, his footsteps behind her, her fingers wrapped around his because she didn't want to let them go. Or him go, even.

And in the end, because she knew he needed to let go, she said, "You could close the door, if you want."

He let her hand go, and the door closed and because she wasn't looking, she didn't see his face.

Until he turned and met her eyes. "Leah, what is this...?"

"I need to get this out," she repeated, drawing the tears and the rest of the emotions she was feeling back inside of her. "I said that I was too busy, that I couldn't spend time with you, be with you for real because I didn't have time. And that was wrong."

She paused, looked at him, watched his face. Watched for *something*.

"It was wrong because it's not about how much time you have but about what you do with it. Because I got a promotion at work, the one I'd wanted. And yet it felt like garbage because I couldn't tell you. And I couldn't call you and I couldn't...because I told you that you didn't mean enough to me to fight."

She heard his sharp intake of breath.

"Fight for us," she continued. "Fight for what you said was bashert. Yes. Bashert, and I see that now."

Silence.

Nothing.

"You probably don't believe me," she said. "And you have every right not to believe me, but—" she gestured toward the wrapped package "—you would probably believe this, something I got for you two weeks before we broke up in high school. I've been carrying it around with me for years now. I haven't opened it. I haven't done anything with it because I couldn't have. I probably always knew I was going to give it to you, watch the expression on your face as you saw what I'd done..."

His jaw was tight, as if he was keeping it from falling and she didn't know what to expect.

She forged ahead anyway. "So this is for you, for the past, for the present and for the future. And for the strings, tangled, tied, invisible, and ones that connect me to you."

She watched, waited as he moved toward the desk, where she'd laid out the package. He cut through and opened the butcher-paper wrapping, slowly revealing and opening what was inside.

"You got me..." he managed, "a print from the hockey comics collaboration they did all those years ago. For graduation."

She nodded, trying desperately to hold back the tears that were threatening to exit out of her, a geyser of unexpected reactions and upsets and nerves.

"Leah," he managed. "You can do anything in the world. You don't have to hide. I'm here. I always have been."

And as he walked toward her, his arms opened, she had the feeling of coming home.

SAMUEL HELD LEAH as she broke down completely in his arms. Upset, angst and nerves turned his shoulder soaking wet.

But he didn't care, not at all. Because she wanted to be there.

"I'm here," he said rubbing the back of her head, letting her cry. "I'm here. Here and now, as long as you want me to be."

"How about forever?"

He smiled up at her. "I think forever might be in the cards. But."

She raised an eyebrow, and there she was, his fighter. "What do you mean but?"

"I brought us something. Something symbolic. Something that says we can write our own story. Together. Starting anew."

She nodded. And his heart was full. "I like that."

And as she opened the paper to reveal the simple frame from his mantel, the simple drawing of white blossoms on snow, framed by a circle of branches.

"You remembered," she said, tracing the ketubahs design with a finger. "An open playing field. Victory after crossing through the brambles and thorns."

"Nobody else's," he said. "But ours."

And then he did the most important thing. He stepped forward, put his arms around her and kissed her.

Hours later, after conversation over a very belated Shabbas dessert and a babka that Shayna had ready to go, he looked up at her. "How about we do this next week, with my family?"

"I like the idea. Not better than babka. But a lot."

And all she could do was laugh, and close his mouth with a kiss that tasted like cinnamon, chocolate, and forever.

The End

Author's Note

There is a LOT to get through here, so let's get to it:

Comic lettering:

There are tons more resources, but these are a few of them. Comic Lettering is a very, very, very specialized art and in order to even write a tiny bit of a conversation about it, I had to learn.

Todd Klein Lettering How To Hand-Lettering (kleinletters.com)
Comic Lettering: How To Start With Lettering a Comic Book | Creative Comic Art

Bad Ink Studios posts some great examples on their TikTok.

JEWS AND COMICS:

History:

After I finished the primary edits on this book, I was invited to Chicago for the Chicago Jewish Book Festival (I cannot speak highly enough about it). Terry Gant gave a wonderful presentation about the history of Jews in Comics, and if you're interested in a really good comic experience, look up his store – Third Coast Comics.

Also one of my favorite Jewish sites in New York, the Center For Jewish History, not only hosted a Jewish Comic Con in 2023 but also hosted an exhibit about the Jewish history of comics, the museum, and Laboratory of the Jewish Comics Experience.

Center for Jewish History :: 15 W. 16th Street NY, NY 10011 (cjh.org)

Present:

Erasure of this Jewish history in contemporary portrayals of comics is a difficult discussion to have, but thankfully it's been had, and is continuing to be had, by people who know more than I do. One of them is Danielle Silverstone. Follow Danielle on Social media, but Danielle is also interviewed as part of this piece from the Washington post.

Why Jewish fans feel erased from Marvel movies (washingtonpost.com)

Posters:

The posters that Samuel worked on were inspired by work created by The Poster Posse. Every single one of these posters are absolutely gorgeous. Go check them out here:

MEOKCA x Poster Posse | Artists & designers who create memorable art for the entertainment industry and many others.

HOCKEY

And comics:

If I were to say that the print that Leah bought and kept for Samuel was inspired by something, it would be the NHL Guardian Project. Created by Stan Lee, the goal was to create a different way of looking at hockey and produced comic style mascot/symbols/heroes based on the NHL teams that existed at the time it was created. If nothing else, it produced some fantastic art work, and for a hockey/sports gal who's trying to find common ground with an aspiring comic guy, this would be perfect. An artist that I adore who was involved in this all those years ago, was Thom Zahler.

Thom Zahler Art Studios
The Guardian Project (comics) – Wikipedia

Women's hockey:

So, I sit a bit more than a month away from the opening of the PWHL, the most recent incarnation of a women's hockey league. I'm rooting for former Riveter Madison Packer. :D I'm also rooting for Abbey Levy, where this story really begins.

But things have happened where I sit that made Leah, and I had concerns about the contract that her client, Carly, would be signing.

The most recent was Mariah Fujimagari, who was released

from a tryout with the Kalamazoo Affiliate of the Detroit Redwings after she was used for both publicity and skills.

Despite Historic Win, Mariah Fujimagari Released from Tryout with Kalamazoo Wings – The ECHL News, Analysis and More (thehockeynews.com)

Sports Agenting:

Whatever I know about sports agenting comes from listening to podcasts and following hockey agents on social media.

But if I had to model how Leah approaches her career/position as a sports agent on someone, it would be Eleni Demestihas. Her story is here:

Getting to Know Eleni Demestihas from Hecate Sports Group (hockeytomorrow.com)

Fictional Sports Teams:

The New York Empires Hockey team comes from the Empires series, written with Isabo Kelly, Laura Hunsacker, Heather Lire, and Cassandra Carr. The beginning of Carly Fein Emerson's journey, as well as the beginning of the Unicorns story, is my contribution to the third anthology, titled Roughing It. The NAWHL, the league Jessica Weiss plays in, also features in the Fifth Question, part of the Hope Connection Anthology of my own shorts.

I know *nothing* about baseball; the Union and the Elephants are part of KD Casey's Unwritten Rules series. References with permission. Also read KD's books. Immediately.

Comic Con:

I've already written about Comic Con from the perspective of a fan, (in What Happens in Comic Con), but I know nothing about how attending as a guest works. Both Jen DeLuca and Celestine Martin generously answered the call and walked me through the behind-the-scenes process of being walked to a panel or a signing as an author. I extrapolated from what they told me in order to create how Samuel was treated his first time out. They are both ridiculously brilliant writers; read their books.

SOFER:

We begin with a conversation about one style of specialized writing, and we end with another.

A softer, writes torahs, ketubahs, mezuzzahs and megillahs—the important scrolls of the Jewish faith. The Hebrew calligraphy a Sofer writes and the routine they use to write the various scrolls is absolutely exquisite. The training is extensive. Here are some of the videos I watched to learn; there are more for sure; these are my favorite. One is an interview by an Australian university student, one is a conversation with an older man who comes to be a sofer later in life, and the other is a female sofer.

youtu.be/a5Brbqgngrc?si=qBRRsqHgeyvhgVf_
youtu.be/kJJ61dVqoFk?si=kYhX18X1TBVURzFM
(1348) Writing the Torah HD – YouTube

Acknowledgements

To Jane Porter, Sinclair Sawhney. Cyndi Parent, V. Walker and Meghan Farrell. Thank you. Thank you for everything you do to make my books better.

To Lynnette Novak for being in my corner, in good times and always.

To Marnie McMahon, Megan Walski, and Felicia Grossman: this book would not ever at all happened without the three of you. You picked me up when I needed it and sat with me as I made magic from this mess. This one was hard and I am so very lucky to have all of you in my corner.

To the New York Commiseration discord crew as well as the Romance Craft Club Discord – thank you.

To Jean Meltzer, Sara Goodman Confino, Heidi Shertok, Meredith Schorr, Felicia Grossman and the rest of the 'Women Talking about Romance Crew'. This has been a beautiful journey. Thank you. May we all go from strength to strength.

To the Romance Schmooze Discord – Kol hakavod, together at every step.

To my Tule Family: I adore you guys – thank you for everything. Always.

To the Chippy Chicks – we have so much fun on Sundays and I absolutely love the time we all spend together.

To the Jewish Bookstagram community – you are all bright beautiful stars, and seeing your posts brings so much joy to my face. Thank you <3

And to any bookstagrammer or blogger, booktoker or publication who took the time to review, talk about, post about any of my books, thank you thank you thank you.

To Raizel and Malya, Leah Jones, the Menchwarmers and all of the other amazing podcasters who had me on to talk Jews and hockey and, romance novels, all the things, thank you.

And to Leah Jones, for inviting me to Chicago and making me smile as I was there, for the joy of the Chicago Jewish Book Festival, Thank you.

To Marisa and Roseann Backlin for hosting me in Chicago and championing my books, thank you :D

To the Ripped Bodice, Meet Cute, 2nd Flight, Transom, The Book Cellar and Sleepy Hollow bookstores, as well as bookstores all over the country and North America for carrying my books and for hosting amazing and fun events. You are important and I appreciate everything you do.

To: Zoe York, Lisa Lin, Deanna Grey, Mia Heintzelman, Sarah Grunder-Ruiz, Alys Murray KD Casey, Felicia Grossman and Lucy Eden <3 thank you all for your friendship AND for celebrating B'Nai Mitzvah and all its facets with me :D

To Marcella Bell, Rebecca Crowley, Kelly Cain, Helena Greer, Rosie Danan, Melonie Johnson Felicia Grossman Meredith Schorr and KD Casey for being part of my Hanukkah series :D

To Kimberly Rocha and the Book Obsessed Chicks – I love all of you.

To Emma Barry, Olivia Dade, Sasha Devlin, NR Lines and so many others who listened to me talk about this book and helped me through it, deserve the world.

Books take villages; some books take more than one. This book took so many villages I do not have a name for all of them. This one was hard and so many people were there for me when I needed it. I learned I have a community with this one, and I will not forget that ever.

To Russ Agdern and Marisa Harford – thank you for everything. And to Elijah, may you see who you will become in Shim now. May he be worthy of you.

And to Jane and Barry Agdern, nothing happens without you. Not this, not anything. I love you both.

If you enjoyed *The Dating Contract*,
you'll love the next book in the…

Last Girls Standing series

Book 1: *B'Nai Mitzvah Mistake*

Book 2: *The Dating Contract*

Available now at your favorite online retailer!

More Books by Stacey Agdern

Friendships and Festivals series

Book 1: *Miracles and Menorahs*

Book 2: *History of Us*

Book 3: *Love and Latkes*

Available now at your favorite online retailer!

About the Author

Stacey Agdern is an award-winning former bookseller who has reviewed romance novels in multiple formats and given talks about various aspects of the romance genre. She incorporates Jewish characters and traditions into her stories so that people who grew up like she did can see themselves take center stage on the page. She's also a member of both LIRW and RWA NYC. She lives in New York, not far from her favorite hockey team's practice facility.

Thank you for reading

The Dating Contract

If you enjoyed this book, you can find more from all our great authors at TulePublishing.com, or from your favorite online retailer.

Milton Keynes UK
Ingram Content Group UK Ltd.
UKHW041905120324
439302UK00005B/321